THE
SEVEN DEADLY SINS

'These seven writers represent . . . a newer and more knowing feminist strategy . . . Mischievous and exhilarating.'

Lorna Sage, *The Observer*

'Rich in experiment and imagination, a sign of just how far contemporary women's writing might go.'

Helen Birch, *City Limits*

'All of these stories cut deeply and with a sharp edge into the main business of life — death, God and the devil.'

Richard North, *New Musical Express*

'A rich but random survey of recent women's writing.'

Jonathan Coe, *The Guardian*

'An exciting, imaginative mix of stories.'

Elizabeth Burns, *The List*

'Witty, modern, female.'

Kathleen Jamie, *Scotland on Sunday*

'Extremely entertaining.'

Emma Dally, *Cosmopolitan*

CONTRIBUTORS

Kathy Acker is the author of *The Childlike Life of the Black Tarantula* (1973), *I Dreamt I was a Nymphomaniac, Imagining!* (1974), *The Adult Life of Toulouse Lautrec* (1975), and *Kathy Goes to Haiti* (1978), all of which are to be reissued in the United States by Grove Press; *Don Quixote* (Paladin); and *Blood and Guts in Highschool, Great Expectations, My Death My Life by Pier Paolo Pasolini* and *Empire of the Senseless*, published here by Picador.

Leslie Dick, who was born in 1954, is an American writer who lives in London. Her first novel, *Without Falling*, was published by Serpent's Tail in 1987, and in the United States by City Lights in 1988.

Zoë Fairbairns was born in 1948. Her published novels include *Benefits* (Virago); *Stand We At Last* (Virago and Pan); *Here Today* (Methuen) — winner of the 1985 Fawcett Book Prize; and *Closing* (Methuen). She is unmarried and so is the man she lives with. When not writing — her main occupation — she runs writing workshops in schools, colleges, prisons, bookshops, Spanish fishing villages, anywhere that invites her, in fact.

Amanda Faulkner is represented by the Angela Flowers Gallery in London. Born in Dorset in 1953, she worked for a time in South America before studying painting at Ravensbourne College of Art, followed by an MA in Printmaking at Chelsea, where she now teaches. She has work in public collections, including the V&A and the Arts Council of Great Britain, and has exhibited widely both in Britain and internationally.

Alison Fell is a novelist and poet. She is the author of *The Grey Dancer, Every Move You Make* and *The Bad Box* (Virago New Fiction), and the poetry collections *Kisses for Mayakovsky* and *The Crystal Owl*. She has also contributed to many anthologies, including *Bread and Roses, Close Company*, and *Truth, Dare or Promise*. One time fiction editor of *Spare Rib*, she has been a writer-in-residence in London and Sydney, and is currently working on a new novel.

Sara Maitland was born in 1950, and now lives in East London. She has published three novels, the most recent of which, *Arky* (Methuen, 1987), is co-written with Michelene Wandor, three collections of short stories, and three works of non-fiction. She has recently edited a collection of women's writings about the 1960s (Virago, 1988), and is currently working on a new novel. Much of what she writes reflects her abiding interest in women's religious experience, particularly in the Western Christian tradition.

Agnes Owens was born in Milngavie, Dumbartonshire in 1926. She has been married twice and has had seven children. Her youngest son was killed in tragic circumstances last December. Originally a shorthand typist, she has worked in shops, factories and as a cleaner. She was encouraged to write after taking a writing class nine years ago, and has published two books, *Gentle Men of the West*, and *Like Birds in the Wilderness*, and has contributed stories to *Lean Tales*.

Michèle Roberts, who is half French, was born in 1949 and lives and works in London. She is co-author of four collections of poetry and two of short stories. She has published four novels, the most recent of which is *The Book of Mrs Noah* (Methuen, 1987) and a solo collection of poetry, *The Mirror of the Mother* (Methuen, 1986). Her poem "Psyche and the hurricane" won a Sotheby's Prize in the Arvon International Poetry Competition 1987.

THE
SEVEN DEADLY SINS

KATHY ACKER
LESLIE DICK
ZOË FAIRBAIRNS
ALISON FELL
SARA MAITLAND
AGNES OWENS
MICHÈLE ROBERTS

with illustrations by
AMANDA FAULKNER

edited by
ALISON FELL

SERPENT'S
TAIL

The publisher thanks Mark Ainley, Martin Chalmers, Bob Lumley, Enrico Palandri, Kate Pullinger, Antonio Sanchez for their advice and assistance.

British Library Cataloguing in Publication Data
The Seven deadly sins.
 I. Fell, Alison   II. Acker, Kathy
 III. Series
 823'.01'08[FS]
 ISBN 1-85242-140-1

First published 1988 by
Serpent's Tail, 4 Blackstock Mews, London N4
Second printing 1989

Typeset by AKM Associates (UK) Ltd, Southall, London

Printed on acid-free paper by
Nørhaven A/S, Viborg, Denmark

CONTENTS

Illustrations by Amanda Faulkner

"It is in order to better develop her moral superiority that woman must gratefully accept the rightful practical domination of man . . . First as a mother, and later as a sister, then above all as a wife, finally as a daughter, and possibly as a maidservant, in these four natural roles woman is designed to preserve man from the corruption inherent in his practical and theoretical existence. Her affective superiority spontaneously confers on her this fundamental office, which social economy develops increasingly by releasing the loving sex from all disturbing cares, active or speculative."

Auguste Comte, *Système de politique positive*

INTRODUCTION

Once upon a time, when a slightly different darkness lay over the land, and ideology was called demonology, the Seven Deadly Sins were born. When the Sins were first grouped together in the early days of Christian monasticism, each one had its corresponding archdemon — Pride to Lucifer, Covetousness to Mammon, Envy to Leviathan, for example. Gradually the arch-demons lost their authority, so that by the time of Thomas Aquinas the Sins appear as independent moral entities. In the guise of animals or secular cavortings, they glower warningly from the choirstalls, tympana, and bestiaries of the time.

The beginning of the 15th century brought the popular spectacle of Morality Plays, in which Everyman, aided by the Seven Cardinal Virtues, wrestles for his immortal soul with these servants of the World, the Flesh and the Devil. When the Reformation split the monolith of the Church, the traditional Moralities gave way to anti-Papist satires and the Sins were put to work, Saatchi-like, for parties; but their moral status remained unquestioned.

And so did their gender. Predictably, the Deadly Sins — all except Lust — were male. Sectarianism aside, it was still Everyman's soul — whether Catholic or Protestant — that the battle was about; Everywoman was nowhere in evidence. Sweetly and effortlessly, woman, when she appears, is Virtue: Meekness, Patience, Abstinence, Industry, Chastity, Charity, Generosity. Otherwise she is Lust, the body rampant. It's the virgin/whore dichotomy, this time inscribed in a crude ethics, but still fencing us in on the familiar territory of the flesh. In areas other than sexual morality, evidently, Everywoman's soul wasn't considered to be at risk. Presumably she was too marginal to be credited with an ethical sense, and thus a capacity for sin . . .

It's a rich patch to play in, then. After so many centuries of upholding Virtue, surely our imaginations contain all the resplendent crimes our history lacks.

In the war of the words other strategists, of course, have been there before us. Brecht, out to demonstrate that all morality is class-based, stood the Sins on their heads in his song cycle *The Seven Deadly Sins of the Lower Middle Classes*, so that they became normal human impulses thwarted by the capitalist command to accumulate. A tactic which seems just as relevant fifty years on, given the ethic of naked greed that the Right —traditional guardians of High Morality — unblushingly advocate!

But I didn't mean to write a manifesto. Ideology is as ideology does, after all, whereas writing will always slither out of any cage you care to put it in.

When I asked six other women writers for fiction pieces, I expected, I suppose, a reclaiming of the Sins in a fairly playful feminist sense. Sara Maitland's heroine in "Gluttony" — a foodie who has every possible rationalization for self-indulgence — certainly falls into this category of grotesque, of modern gargoyle, but elsewhere there are as many approaches as there are authors.

Collaging male gay texts with fragments from city life, Kathy Acker's "Lust" stages an assault on the canons of authorship and identity, as well as on fixed notions of sexual morality and gender. By contrast, Agnes Owens opts for realism in her everyday tale of Scottish redundancy, where "Pride" is a single mother determined to keep her standards up.

In what is almost a moral fable, Zoë Fairbairns shows Everywoman — in the guise of an up-and-coming writer — taunted and tempted by the forces of Covetousness, whereas Leslie Dick delves into psychoanalytic theory to create archetypes of Envy: a childless woman erects barricades of impossibility between herself and the pregnancy she longs for; a malevolent succubus smothers herself in her cot just to spite her mother.

Michèle Roberts creates a narrative of prejudice in which Anger is mis-recognized and mis-attributed, before finally erupting as aberrant symptom once a month.

If some of the characters in the stories rebel against confining roles, others try to erect safe boundaries. In my own story, Sloth and Industry are two sisters who must stake out opposing territories — fat and thin, active and passive — simply to differentiate themselves.

Independently of the stories, Amanda Faulkner's drawings bring the Sins home to roost in the body. Pride, for example, sprouts rows of jewelled breasts; paranoid Envy looks everywhere but at what she has; Anger is literally in fragments, punishing herself. Far from being victims, these women relish their sins, but have enough self-irony to know just what they're doing.

The stories weave in and out of forms, overlap, while the drawings let the sins under our skin in a different way again. Fairy story and feminist gothic, realism and deconstructive writing: all of these have their place if we're out to subvert the patriarchal order. And of course so we are, and so we do, but that isn't the whole picture. It's never just a matter of expropriating the appropriators, after all, but of writing ourselves some decent parts.

Alison Fell

THE
SEVEN DEADLY SINS

ANGER

MICHÈLE ROBERTS

ANGER

"The Story of Melusine"

ANGER

Once upon a time, there was a redhaired countrywoman called Bertrande living with her husband, Guillaume Tarentin, in their small house tucked into the side of a steep hill in Provence. Further down the pebbly track which led as far as their stone porch and nowhere else was a small orchard of apple and apricot trees, and, beyond that, quite a way down, two or three other small houses in which their neighbours lived. Right at the bottom of the hill was the village itself. Guillaume always said he liked living so high up, on account of the peace and quiet. The neighbours said it was so Bertrande could shout at him without anybody hearing. The neighbours added that Bertrande also liked being able to look down her big nose at everyone else.

This was literally true. When she hung the washing out in the mornings, the neighbours, if they craned their necks, could see her look up at the vast sky over her head, gaze at the hillside sheering on up above her, and then stare down at the roofs of their own houses. She had an odd rigid posture always, and at these moments would wrap her fists in her apron. Then up onto tiptoe she would go, still staring down at them, until you would have thought her legs and feet must be made of wood.

Guillaume was well-off by village standards. He and Bertrande could afford to eat their own produce, once the landlord had taken his share, not just sell it all and subsist on bread and root vegetables as the very poorest did. They ate eggs from their own chickens, and killed and boiled the same fowls when these got too old for laying; they could afford to buy olive oil to dip their bread into; if they only ate roast meat on big feast days well at least they could afford bones for soup; and Bertrande, like all the women of the village, was skilled at stretching a little a long way. What was left over from one day got turned into something else the next. Likewise, she had the knack of making clothes and utensils out of odd materials. The ticking that covered her goose-feather quilts served also to make shirts and chemises for herself and her husband; earthenware flowerpots held her wooden spoons and spatulas and tin ladles; she cut up bits of old felt to make slippers and boots. She saved everything, and found a use for it. Bits of string, knotted together, mended chair seats and baskets; she grew flowers in old saucepans, which she then stuck in a row on the windowsill; out of old boxes she made cupboards and stools; out of old cardboard she made patches for broken windows, mats for the kitchen floor of trodden earth, trays on which to store vegetables.

Thrift and good housekeeping were all very well, the neighbours thought, but Bertrande went too far. She was seen at Mass with chicken feathers, not ribbons, stuck in her shawl for decoration. The holy water stoup hung from a nail in the kitchen held salt. Surely her cheeks were sometimes redder than nature intended? Why, even in summer, did she swaddle herself in long heavy clothes and shiver? Why, when she came down to the village once a week for market, was she sometimes heard singing songs that no one else knew? Sometimes she did not come down at all, and it was Guillaume who had to take her place, with his heavy baskets of fruit and vegetables, amongst the other women. Kindly, they looked away from him, and only shrugged to one another. They knew that when Bertrande should have been about her work in house and garden she was sometimes to be seen wandering on the hillside collecting wild flowers. Not to dry them for tisanes, oh no; she pressed them, stuck them on squares of sugar paper, and hung them on the wall. They felt sorry for her husband and were not surprised when after the market packed up he would vanish into the dark little village bar and get roaring drunk before staggering back up the hill.

Bertrande's hands were the largest of any woman's in the village, broad and red, marked with chilblains in winter, seamed with dirt in spring, often puckered with scars and scorch blisters, for she was clumsy in her work much of the time, didn't seem to learn from mistakes. Fresh sore patches kept reappearing as soon as the last lot healed. Once she appeared at market with a purple bruise spreading from one cheekbone up across her eye. Oh, I banged myself, she said with her hoarse laugh. Her hands were capable though, when they wanted to be. When it was a question of money. Her hands could gesture well when she wanted to drive a hard bargain over the price of her fat sweet tomatoes; her hands could seize and wring a goose's neck in seconds; her hands could force open a goose's stubborn beak and stuff it with grain to fatten it well; her hands could slaughter ducks and butcher lambs; her thick fingers could sort coins into shining piles of silver in a twinkling. But what you never saw Bertrande's hands doing was caressing a child. Married for ten years, she appeared incapable of conceiving an heir.

The neighbours pitied Bertrande for this calamity. They conceded the pride that would not let her discuss it, even while they deplored it. They were ready to offer suggestions and remedies, but Bertrande refused to talk about it. She hardly spoke to them at all. This was odder than ever, the neighbours thought, when you considered that Bertrande was well known, in other ways, to be a noisy woman. She suffered from bad dreams at night, they knew, for she often woke her neighbours with her yells. They could hear her nag her husband when he came home drunk; her screams carried down the hillside. She quarrelled with Guillaume frequently for no good reason; the neighbours, pruning their apple trees or digging their vegetable plots, could hear her cursing him in her guttural voice. They were used to the racket she made.

So when at last she fell pregnant, and turned even more sullen and quiet with them, the village women were not so much relieved as worried. They hadn't noticed her belly swelling for a good few months, hidden as it was under her heavy black clothes. When they did, and joked with her about it, she flinched away, grumbling. She wouldn't accept offers of help and advice from the other women, who were hurt by this. At last they could welcome her as one of themselves, yet she snubbed every attempt at friendliness. Once, the midwife, meeting her in the little cemetery next to the church, reached out and patted Bertrande's belly, and the younger woman turned on her and hissed.

Everyone knew, of course, that Bertrande had come to live with her husband from a far-off village, right over the other side of the hill. So they were prepared to make certain allowances for a stranger, and indeed, they always had. And pregnant women were known to behave oddly, to have strange fancies, to crave strange foods. But this behaviour was too proud and angry to pass unnoticed. So the anxious village women began to watch her even more closely.

In her fifth month of pregnancy, Bertrande was spotted in the woods digging up certain roots that were well known to bring on young women's monthly flows, and indeed were prescribed by the midwife for just this reason. In her sixth month of pregnancy, Bertrande was observed helping her husband in their upper field to clear it of rocks and boulders preparatory to ploughing: she picked up the heaviest possible rocks and lugged them to the edge of the hill, where it sheered off into a steep cliff, and tipped them over one by one, grunting like a pig with the effort. That Sunday, after Mass, the priest remonstrated with Guillaume. He should not let his wife roam so far from home into the woods to collect roots that could do her harm if she ate them. He should not have decided to clear the upper field, at last, at just this time. Certainly his wife's labour was essential to his making a living, no one would dispute that, but still, there were limits that should not be passed. Guillaume listened, and sighed. Then he beckoned his wife over from where she stood grumpy and silent among the other women, and took her back up the hill. That night, for the first time since the young couple had come to live there, the neighbours heard the sound of sobbing coming from Guillaume's house.

In her seventh and eighth months, Bertrande seemed calmer.

She still spoke little, but she went about her usual work with her old doggedness, and was even heard once or twice singing some of her peculiar songs. But in the lulls at market, when customers were few and there was a chance to gossip and relax, she did not occupy herself stitching clothes for the baby. What are you going to wrap it in? the other women asked her: one of those old sacks you're so fond of making cushions out of? a piece of cardboard? Bertrande threw her arms in the air and laughed loudly, and a kitchen knife fell out of her sleeve and clattered on the cobblestones under the market stall.

The baby came two weeks early, on midwinter night. The midwife, sweating up the hill through the deep snow, got to the house to find two of the neighbours sitting with the labouring woman, one on each side of her big bed, and their husbands offering Guillaume tots of potato brandy in the kitchen below. Each time his wife cried out, Guillaume drank another glass of brandy. Tears ran out of the corners of his red-rimmed eyes, and he crashed his fists onto the tabletop in time to the rhythm of the shouts from above. The midwife bathed Bertrande's face, and encouraged her. Outside, the snow fell. The men stoked the fire in the kitchen, and crouched over it, hating that room above and the pain in it. They kicked the dogs who whined to get closer to the warm red flames, and they played cards, and drank potato brandy until they fell asleep and did not have to listen any more. The newborn's thin wail interrupted their dreams of suffering, and they woke, and looked at each other blearily, then got up clumsily and knelt down on the cold mud floor and thanked God.

Guillaume went shyly upstairs to see his son. The son, however, was a daughter.

Never mind, his two friends consoled him when he came back downstairs: better luck next time. We'll drink her health anyway.

The midwife, who was like most of the others a kind woman when she could afford to be, came every day to see Bertrande and the child, as did the two neighbours, who made pots of lentil soup and cleaned the house and kept the fire going while the three men dug paths through the snow to the stables and saw after the animals. The women clucked and shook their heads over Bertrande's housekeeping arrangements. Never before, they remonstrated with each other, had they known such a slut, one who kept a stack of wax crayons and a drawing-book in her larder, whose linen chest contained a litter of chestnuts and corks and dried berries threaded on strings, who had decorated the wall behind the privy with her own finger and palm prints, and who had hidden a pack of Tarot cards at the bottom of the flour bin. Still, they were so happy running their fingers through worn patches in the best towels, and examining the top of the high mantelpiece for dust, and wondering whether the inky scrawls on bits of paper stuffing the draughty gaps in the windows were spells or illicit love letters, that when they went up to the bedroom to check how the new mother was doing they were in a cheerful frame of mind and could be patient with her.

For Bertrande found it very difficult to feed her baby. Indeed, the women whispered, you could say she didn't want to. She needed a lot of encouragement to do it, and it seemed that even when she did her milk was thin and did not adequately nourish the baby, who cried a lot in a fretful sort of way that was hard to bear. Still, the baby, who at first had seemed weak and sickly, was at least surviving. In no time at all, the women counselled Bertrande, in a couple of days, say, the little one would take to the breast without such fuss, and then the milk would flow more easily and Bertrande would relax and all would be well.

The crying drove Guillaume from the house, you could see that. He could be of little use, of course, for the women were there with his wife doing everything, and it was not a man's place anyway. He took to neglecting even the jobs he could have been doing in that bad weather, bits of mending and glueing and general re-fixing, and the house grew even more tumbledown around him. He did the bare minimum for the animals, then slouched out, saying he was going down to the neighbours to see if they needed him for anything. The two husbands reported that they never saw him. It was clear that he slipped and slithered down the snowy path to the village bar most evenings, for he would return just as the two women were about to leave for their own homes, wet through and smelling of brandy. He was suffering, but no one could ask him why, for that was not their way. No one had words for what was going on, and they never had had. The priest might have had words for it, but he never came up the hill in the bad weather, and the women did not dare suggest that Guillaume go and visit him. They watched Bertrande turn her head away when her husband came into the bedroom and hovered by the cradle, they saw her look contemptuously at him as he slunk out, they saw her mouth set hard and her big red hands make lumpy fists under the sheet. She wouldn't say the rosary with them of an evening. She wouldn't let them touch the baby with holy water in case the devil carried its soul away before they got it down to the church for a christening. Yet it was well known that these practices were efficacious. The women sighed. With such a mother, what prospect was there for the child?

After a week, there came a thaw. The two husbands took it as a signal to call their wives home, where they were much needed, and the midwife departed to a nearby village to attend another lying-in.

Bertrande and Guillaume were left alone with each other and the baby.

When the thing happened, it took a while for the villagers to make sense of it. As the neighbours explained to the people living lower down the hill, Guillaume was in such a state of anxiety when he came sliding down the muddy track to their door that for a while they could get nothing out of him, only curses and weeping. They gave him brandy, and that steadied him. Then he told them. But even then he was so incoherent and muddled that his worried listeners had to piece his story together for themselves, and, once the news had flown down the hill and began to be passed round the village, no one could be quite sure of the right order of Guillaume's words any more, let alone what had actually happened.

Guillaume said the fire was out. No, Bertrande said that the fire was out. She was cold, and so was the baby. She needed fire. She needed to be warm. She wanted to go back to bed, not to sit in a cold kitchen with no fire. Guillaume went out to the shed to fetch wood for the fire. The fire was not out. The fire was near Bertrande. Bertrande was near the fire. She made more fire with the poker. The flames licked up. She held the baby to the fire to make it warm, like the fire inside her. She held the fire to the baby. Bertrande dropped the baby in the fire. She said it was not an accident.

Later, the priest tried to sort out the right words. Bertrande. The baby fell in the fire by accident.

But everyone knew that that was not really true. And the priest was not there so how could he know? And Bertrande was never seen in church again, so it was clear she had not made her confession: he had not found out that way.

The child lived. Miraculously, the women said, crossing themselves, her little face was unscathed when Guillaume picked her off the glowing embers and tore the smouldering wrappings off. Though she had been dropped face downwards, only the skin on the uppermost part of her body had been touched by the red ashes burning through. Though the new skin would grow again, it would be shiny and angry and red. But she would not die.

The priest came puffing up the hill to christen the child. They named her Melusine. No one knew where the name came from, and no one dared ask. Guillaume simply said that it would be so. Bertrande went to bed and stayed there and was silent. They brought the child to her to be fed, and they watched her to make sure that she did not try to harm it again. Downstairs in the kitchen, drinking unhappy toasts to the bandaged newborn, they whispered to each other that Bertrande was a monster.

After that, the midwife sent for her sister, who was unmarried, to come and keep house for Guillaume and to keep an eye on Bertrande, who remained in bed and would not get up. Nor would she speak to anyone. Luckily, the midwife's sister was a cheerful girl, who was not affected by the atmosphere in the house. She did not mind drunken men, being used to them, and when one night, on returning from the village bar, Guillaume pulled open the front of her blouse, she only giggled a bit. She told her sister all about it, and her sister told her to be careful. People would talk.

Bertrande would not talk. She heard the whisperings, the women knew, which sidled up through the floorboards, down the chimney, in at the window: they did not always bother to lower their voices. It was right she should know what they thought.

They always said the same thing. They watched the words settle inside her, souring her stomach so that she could not eat or drink. They watched the words gnaw at her soul, worrying at it, shredding it to rags and holes. They watched her feed what was left of her soul into her daughter's rosy mouth which ardently sucked it in. The baby seemed to use up her mother's strength: she flourished, while Bertrande grew weaker day by day. Or perhaps, the women whispered, the devil was claiming his own. You could see how Bertrande did not resist him; she drifted easily towards her death. Guillaume slept in the kitchen now. One morning, awakened early by the baby's cries, he stumbled upstairs to rouse his wife to feed her, and found Bertrande cold and stiff against the big square pillow. Her hair, he told the neighbours later, was unplaited and loose all round her face, and there was a thick strand of it caught between her lips.

The priest decided that since Bertrande had not been arraigned and convicted of any crime, charity dictated that she be buried in the corner of the churchyard, close enough to the church to be included in the company of the righteous, and at a sufficient distance not to cause offence. It was a poor funeral, people said afterwards: like a pauper's. They understood why Guillaume would not allow any flowers, and why he did not invite them back to his house afterwards, and why he marked the grave with a plain cross made of cheap wood with no words cut on it other than his wife's name. What else could he have done? Bunched in their best black, separated from him by six feet of respect, they watched him stand, pale and dry-eyed, at the grave's edge, while the priest read out the words of prayers that were snatched from his mouth by the wind and soon lost.

Then Guillaume needed a new wife. He needed her hands labouring in the kitchen and the fields and the garden, he needed her broad back to help him bear his sorrow and shame, he needed her cunt in his bed at night. He needed her eyes never to look into his in the way that Bertrande's had. So, since his friends and the priest went on at him that he should regularize the position in which the midwife's sister found herself, he seduced her properly and then married her. Everybody agreed it was for the best. The wetnurse jiggled Melusine up and down in her arms, and the plump redhaired baby laughed with pleasure.

Melusine must always have known, Pierre Caillou thought, the story of her mother's life and death. It must have grown her, have shaped her. But it was not this old scandal that made him notice her particularly: he grew interested in Melusine only when he first realized she had a secret.

Pierre Caillou was the village schoolmaster. He was an educated man, who had left the village to study fifty kilometres away in the great city none of his compatriots had ever seen, and who had returned full of ideas and compassion, determined to give his neighbours' children the chance to learn how to read and write and to lead better lives than those of their parents. After five years of trying to run an elementary school on proper scientific lines, he admitted defeat, acquired a stooped back, and contented himself with teaching those children whose parents let them attend school when they were not needed in the fields or in the house. He had a lot of free time, with so few scholars. So he became himself a student again, first of local folklore and superstition, and then, more precisely, of the customs, morals and beliefs of his fellow villagers. They resented him for this, and he did not blame them. He knew he was privileged, doing no physical work, and with his schoolmaster's stipend topped up by the rents from two farms he had inherited from his parents. He had no friends, though he occasionally played backgammon with the priest on those nights when loneliness drove him to accept the old curé's stupid tolerance of his atheism. He slept at the school, on a truckle bed set up in his office. At night he would extinguish the fire, bundle himself in a grey woollen blanket, and scribble in his notebook. He had a row of these on the mantelpiece, all identical, cheap flimsy notebooks bound in brown cloth.

At fourteen years old, Melusine was still coming to school each morning. It kept her out of mischief, Guillaume said to Pierre, shrugging his shoulders, it kept her from getting in the way, and if she picked up some useful knowledge, well, all to the good. She could do his accounts for him and prove her usefulness that way. Madame Tarentin agreed: these days, people needed a bit of booklearning. And Melusine already knew most of what there was to know about tending a house. She could afford to put in some time at school. She could help her parents in the afternoons, when the school was closed.

Melusine always sat in the corner of the classroom, near the black iron stove, the best place because the warmest, which she had won on account of being the oldest scholar, and a position she defended with kicks and biting when necessary. Yet she also liked it, Pierre Caillou thought, because the angle of the wall and the bulge of the stove cut her off from the other children, and because she could look out of the window beside her at the short row of pollarded limes edging the path up to the church and watch the comings and goings of people and animals and birds. She daydreamed a lot, and he often had to reprove her, for her inattention was an affront to his authority over the other children. Yet she was a good student: she could read and write well, unlike most of the others, and she was quick at sums when she put her mind to it.

One day he spied on her from behind, peering over her shoulder before she could run the sponge over her slate. He had set the children a geography test, commanding them to draw a map of their province complete with rivers and towns. But Melusine had chosen to sketch, in her coloured chalks, the portrait of some mythical creature she must have seen in a picture book somewhere: a wild being of the woods, half-man, half-beast, covered from head to toe in thick curly fur, and with little breasts peeping out that proved her to be female.

—What's this? Pierre Caillou asked, reaching his hand over Melusine's shoulder and grabbing her slate.

He moved round in front of her in order to see her face. It was dreamy and contented; she was still in her daydream, her pleasure. He realized that she was not as ugly as he had always thought. It was when she was afraid that she grew ugliness as an extra and protective skin. Still absorbed in her drawing, still attached to it, she was soft, shining.

—Where did you copy this from? he persisted: where did you find it?

Melusine hesitated.

—Nowhere, she said: I just drew it.

He reached for the sponge. She watched him. She was impassive, hard again. He touched the sponge to the slate. Her face twitched.

—In the mirror, she blurted: I saw it in the mirror.

—Stay behind at twelve o'clock, he commanded: I want to get to the bottom of this.

It was cold in the little office where he slept. Melusine stood by the open door, shivering. Noticing, he gestured her in, shut the door behind her, and lit the fire. Normally he never permitted himself a fire in the morning. Only ever at night.

He sat on the truckle bed and she stood in front of him where he ordered her to stand.

—Take your clothes off, he said: show me.

Melusine frowned.

—Don't be silly, he scolded: I am your teacher, there can be nothing wrong. Do as I tell you.

She stood, stiff, between his knees. So he undressed her himself, laying her black school overall carefully on the bed beside him, undoing the buttons of her smock one by one, tugging the rough linen chemise over her head, till he had her naked to the waist.

He knew, of course, as did everyone in the village, that she had been burnt as a baby, and that the midwife had said that the skin would grow back but would be shiny and puckered and red, that she would be grotesque in the place where the women of that country were smooth milky white. What he had not expected were the little breasts. He had thought her too young. What he had not expected was the thick, silky thatch of bright red hair that curled from her neck down around her breasts and on down to her waist.

He stretched his hand out. It shook a little. He touched the red mat of hair, and then her breasts, first one and then the other. Melusine tried to step backwards and he gripped her between his knees.

—Don't be frightened, he told her: I won't hurt you.

He suddenly found that he wanted her to want his caresses. He had never touched a woman before. He wanted her to unbend towards him, as though he were the fire and she could warm herself at him.

—Melusine, he demanded: when did this happen?

She hung her head and mumbled. Even when he laid her gently on the bed and lifted up her skirts, she said nothing he could understand.

—I'll take you home, he decided afterwards: I must speak to your father about this.

The Tarentins were obliged to ask him in to share their midday meal. All the time he was reaching for more bread, or accepting a second plate of cabbage soup, or wiping his greasy mouth on the back of his hand, he was watching Melusine, who sat at the far end of the table and of course said nothing. In those days children did not speak in front of their elders, and Pierre Caillou approved of this. It allowed him to speak of Melusine as though she were not there. His questions, however, alarmed Madame Tarentin, and she sent her stepdaughter outside to sweep the yard. For a moment he saw Melusine's moon face glimmer sadly at the little window; then her father shook his fist at the glass and she disappeared.

Some months before, the parents told him, Melusine was discovered scrubbing herself under the pump, trying to get rid of the unsightly growth of hair that had appeared overnight on the scarred skin of her chest. At the same time they had not only caught her rootling in the old wooden chest into which Bertrande's things had been thrown after her death, but had discovered that she had used the stubs of wax crayon she found there to produce drawings of a hideous sort. No amount of beatings administered by her worried father could stop her drawing. No amount of herbal poultices applied by her worried stepmother could get rid of the thick growth of hair. In the end they used Guillaume's cut-throat razor and shaved it off. But the hair had simply grown back the next month, and she had gone on making her drawings on every scrap of cardboard she could lay her hands on. The most disturbing aspect of the whole business, the parents admitted, was that the hair regularly disappeared of its own accord after four or five days, and re-appeared with equal regularity a month later. Bertrande, that unhappy woman, and here they both crossed themselves, had delivered herself of a monster.

Pierre Caillou and Melusine were married soon afterwards, just as soon as the banns had been properly read and Melusine had finished hemming the last sheet and nightgown in her trousseau which, like all the girls in the village, she had started sewing at an early age. She didn't bring Pierre Caillou much, for her parents had little money to spare that winter, and he used this fact to put pressure on them to agree to the marriage. They were relieved, he could see, to get their daughter settled with the only man in the village who could possibly have accepted her.

—Now she's got you to look after her, Madame Tarentin told him: she'll be all right at last. I shan't have to worry about what will become of her any more.

—It's all right, she should marry and go with you, Guillame said: poor thing.

They made only one condition. Pierre must promise never to look at his wife unclothed during the period each month when the hair grew on her chest and around her breasts, for this would shame her too much and so halt her chances of living some sort of normal married life. And perhaps, Madame Tarentin added, if he allowed her at those times of seclusion to do the drawing and painting she so loved, she would grow reconciled to her deformity and fret about it less.

For several months Pierre Caillou was happy with his new wife. She spoke little, it was true, but he was used to silence, having lived alone for so long, and found her taciturnity a relief rather than a problem. Her stepmother had trained Melusine well: she could cook, sew and clean quite adequately, and she did not complain about the cold and the draughts in the disused classroom they began to use as a bedroom, nor did she nag him for more housekeeping or new clothes. He was able to go on living much as he always had; she did not grudge him the books he sent for from the bookshops in the city, nor the pipes of tobacco he smoked at night when writing up his notes. He knew that she needed greatly to please him, to show her gratitude that he had taken her on, and he argued with himself that this was quite right, for had he not rescued her from a life of miserable loneliness? The villagers might gossip about them for a while, might indulge their curiosity about the new menage for as long as it took them to become bored with the young couple's obvious blamelessness and contentment, but in time the whispers and sniggers would die down. His neighbours had not, he knew, expected him to marry. He took a certain pleasure in walking with Melusine on Sunday afternoons up and down the village street, and watching the looks cast at his wife's freshly ironed Sunday gown, at her neat coil of red hair under her bonnet, at the scrubbed pair of sabots she kept for best, at her large blue eyes demurely cast down and her wide mouth firmly closed over her sharp little teeth. She was as comely, on these occasions, as any other girl in the village, and he prided himself on the fact that she was also far more intelligent.

He taught her to keep a certain distance. He would not allow her to attend Sunday Mass, for he wanted to wean her from superstition and bigotry, and he did not allow her to climb the hill to visit her parents more than once every two months, for he wanted to give her a chance to lead her own life and become independent of peasant ways. At night she practised reading, writing and spelling under his supervision, and she soon proved herself skilled enough to take dictation, when he needed to think aloud, and to make fair copies into manuscript from his notebooks. Nor did he forget his promise to her parents: when the hair around her breasts came each month he sent her to sleep on his old truckle bed which was set up at these times in the pantry beyond the kitchen at the back of the schoolroom. He let her keep her paints and paper there and retire early, on what he called her red nights, to mess about to her heart's content with water and colours by the light of a tallow candle. After five nights of sleeping separately, she would return, docile and quiet, to his bed, and to any caresses he felt like making. When he asked to see her paintings she looked cross and shook her head at first, but when he threatened to enter her sanctum and fetch them himself she instantly complied. He was surprised at how well this untaught peasant girl could paint, and praised her unstintingly. He spoke to her of the art galleries in the cities he had visited in his days as a student, and her eyes gleamed as she listened. He sent for volumes of engravings, and explained composition to her, and she smiled her rare smile. He knew that he was ignorant of love in the way that his fellow students had practised it, for he had been much too shy to visit brothels with them. He knew that he was ignorant of love in the way that the men in the village practised it, for he suspected them of being animals who treated their wives as holes in the ground to be pissed into and made pregnant year after year. Melusine suited him, for she needed him and looked up to him. So as well as studying her peculiarities he began to love her, and to hope that she loved him in return.

· He began to look forward to the evening, to the clock on the mantelpiece chiming seven-thirty, the hour at which he cleared his books off the table and Melusine in her stout calico apron came in to lay the cloth and then brought in the steaming tureen of delicious soup. Afterwards, as she sat sewing in the chair opposite his, or perched next to him at the table and copied out notes under his direction, he would look at her big forehead, her capable square-tipped fingers, her downcast eyes, and want her to look back at him. He began to want to know what went on in her mind.

But she would not respond in the way he wanted. Where he hoped for naïve confidences, for the revelations of her fresh young heart, he got stories she had picked up from her parents as a child, or details of recipes, or gossip overheard on their Sunday walks together. Melusine, it appeared, was not so very different from the other women in the village after all. She was not, after all, original. She told him nothing he could not have heard himself at the baker's or the butcher's or the bar. Even at night, when he lay in her arms after they had made love in the way he liked best, he could not catch her off-guard. She would say she was sleepy, turn over, and hide her eyes from him.

So he began to think about her secret again. It was here, he concluded, that the core of her personality lay. Hadn't he always known that, right from that first day when he caught her drawing in the classroom? So he began to question her, timidly at first and then with growing confidence, about how she felt about the thick growth of hair that came and went every month around her breasts, about how she felt about the stories concerning her mother that were still rife in the village, about how she felt on those nights when she sat in the pantry by the light of her tallow candle and painted the pictures she saw inside herself. Wasn't he right that there were some paintings she never showed him, that she kept secret? But Melusine just looked at him blankly, and shrugged. Or she would kiss him, to quieten him that way. Or, if they were in bed together, she would begin to fondle him in the expert way she had developed. He began to wish she had not learned so well how to please him. Yet he liked being pleased by her, and the more he liked it the more he grew desperate to be sure she loved him and was not just doing her duty.

But the more he pestered her to talk about her secret feelings and thoughts, the more he begged her to show him *all* her paintings, the more Melusine grew silent, irritable and finally rebellious. She said *no* frequently. She kept the key of the pantry door in her pocket. And at the same time he was forced to notice that not only had she developed the habit of littering the kitchen and their bedroom with pictures and drawings and rough sketches, she had also begun to spend more nights shut away from him each month. Five nights at first, then six, then seven, then eight. And the villagers, who liked to pop in and out of the school and see how Melusine and Pierre were getting on, began to notice that Melusine was turning out as undomestic as her mother had been. The villagers began to whisper and giggle about a husband who could not control his eccentric wife. Pierre Caillou, who had always insisted that he didn't care a damn about gossip, began to suffer.

Some days Melusine was late cooking supper, and held a sketch in one hand while she served crisp fried potatoes with the other. Sometimes, on a Sunday, she neglected to put on her pretty clothes and complained she didn't want to take a walk with her husband, she'd rather stay indoors and draw. Often at night now she made love to him in such a brisk perfunctory fashion that he felt used, and that she was rushing the love-making so as to be done with it and sleep.

When, one month, Melusine returned to his bed after nine nights in the pantry, Pierre enquired whether the cause of her strange behaviour were perhaps that she were pregnant? Melusine laughed: no. Was she ill? Would she see the doctor? No.

He wondered whether she had taken a lover in secret, whether she lay in the pantry with some red-faced peasant and cuckolded him month after month. No, Melusine said. Laughing at him before she turned away to swill a plate covered with dried smears of blue and green paint.

He started staying awake at night, so that he could stare at her as she slept, and try to wrest her secret from her closed eyelids or the low words she sometimes muttered as she dreamed. He followed her about the house as she expertly swept and scrubbed, watching the stoop of her broad back, the dexterity of her wrists. He tried to trick her in the evenings, shooting sudden questions at her. He examined the chest where she kept her clothes mixed up with a rubbish of dried flowers and chicken feathers and withered chestnuts. He grew thin with worry, and sometimes forgot to shave in the mornings. He knew he was behaving strangely, and was frightened because he had no control over himself any more. He told Melusine more and more often how much he loved her, but all she would do was pat him on the arm or cuddle him as though he were a child seeking reassurance and then turn away to her housework or her drawing.

On the tenth night of the following month, Melusine had still not returned to his bed. He lay shaking under the grey woollen blankets, and tried to put his worry outside himself so that he could see it and name it and conquer it. Then he realized that he wasn't simply jealous about his wife's passion for spending increasing amounts of time away from him locked in the pantry getting up to unknown mischief. No. He was deeply concerned for her health and well-being. Here the fear leapt up and growled at him. His whole body trembled, but he forced himself to go on thinking. If the hair around Melusine's breasts were staying on her body for a longer time each month, did that not logically suggest that there would come a time when his wife would be disfigured by the hair *every* day of *every* month? And supposing the hair went on growing until it had completely covered her body? Had he married a real wild woman of the woods, half-human and half-beast, of the sort the villagers whispered about when telling tales around their fires at night? *Was* she truly a monster, as her parents had hinted?

He leapt up, dragged on his dressing-gown and shoved on his slippers, and went to his office, to the rows of books on his shelves dealing with myth, with anthropology, with fairy stories. With metamorphosis and changelings and werewolves. His fingers ran from index to index, from tome to tome. And he read right through all the notebooks in which for so many years now he had carefully recorded all the superstitions and folkloric customs of the primitive people he lived among.

He lifted his head, surprised by a change in the light. His tallow candle was burning low, and a grey glimmer in the dark sky met his eyes when he pushed open the shutters of the window and leaned out to gulp in the sweet, cold night air. It would soon be dawn. It would soon be breakfast time. Soon, his wife would serenely emerge from her hiding-place and rake out the stove before laying and lighting a fire and boiling a pan of water for coffee.

He walked into the kitchen, and saw that a gold crack of light showed under the pantry door. Then he knew what he had to do. It was very simple. He told himself he was not breaking his promise to Melusine's parents. Things had gone too far for worrying about keeping promises. He had a right to know what his wife got up to night after night on her own in there. He had a right to know whether her chest was still covered with hair after ten nights of seclusion. He had a right to know whether he had unwittingly married a monster.

So he banged on the door. Silence. He rattled the door-knob. Silence. Trying to open the door, he found it was indeed locked. So he knelt down and peered in through the keyhole.

The pantry was ablaze with light. Standing in the centre of the tiny room, leaning one hand on the table, was the most beautiful woman Pierre had ever seen. She was naked. She was tall, and creamy skinned, and her long red hair flowed down her back like streams of fire. There was no blemish anywhere on her. She turned her head and smiled at someone he could not see, someone standing just outside his line of vision. Her lips moved, and she spoke. He could not hear her words, nor could he, squinting, make out their shape by lip-reading. Then she turned her head and looked straight at the door.

He roused the neighbours with his screams. When finally they broke the pantry door down, the candles had been blown out, leaving only the harsh smell of tallow, and there was no one in the room. All Melusine's painting equipment had vanished. On the table there lay only a bundle of red-stained rags.

The footprints in the earth of the flowerbed under the school's pantry window could also be traced in the muddy ruts of the village street. Some people said they stopped at the fishpond. Others said they led towards the river. Still others said they went towards the disused well beside the church. No one could be sure.

As the news of Melusine's disappearance spread, reports began to come in from neighbouring villages, brought by men and women who had never met her and knew her only as the daughter of Bertrande.

There was a redhaired woman patient in the lunatic asylum at St Remy. A redhaired woman had been seen boarding the train for Aix. A redhaired prostitute in Marseilles had recently aborted a son with two heads. The painters down from Paris for the

summer at Oppede-le-Vieux had a redhaired woman amongst
them. There was a redhaired monster lady in the freak show
travelling the coast.

None of the villagers could imagine where Melusine had gone.

Dead people go to Purgatory, to have all the badness burnt out of
them by a great fire. But the fire happens when you are born, not
after you are dead.

We love each other so much. You hold me in your arms, you
kiss my breasts, here, here, then you kiss my belly and in between
my legs. We will always be faithful to each other. I will hold your
hand palm down on the top of the stove until you swear never to
leave me.

I kiss and lick all of your skin between your neck and your
waist. I am crying because I love you so much. My tears fall on you
and are warm on your scars.

When you drink too much I will beat you.

When I drink too much I will beat you.

Now we can have a baby. I am you and you are me. Out of the
fire between us comes the baby.

The fire is in the kitchen, its flames leaping high. The mother is
in the kitchen, tending the fire and the baby.

I can come into the kitchen to warm myself at the fire as often
as I want, and the mother will never turn me away. After I am
married I shall keep coming back to the kitchen, to warm myself
at her red hands.

Look in the mirror, the mother says, and see how beautiful you
are. Silly, you're holding the mirror in the wrong place. Hold it
lower down. See the red fire glowing there, in the secret place
between your legs. See how beautiful you are. You are like me.
You are my daughter. I will love you forever. You can leave me
and you can always come back.

I have branded you with the mark of my love. You are my red
baby.

Out of the love between us comes the fire, and the warm kitchen and the mother in the kitchen. Every time we make the fire, we make the kitchen, and the mother.

You can love me, and you can love your mother. You do not have to choose between us.

I shall get married in the kitchen. My mother dropped me in the fire, but she will heal me. She will heal me with her tears.

I shall love you forever and I shall not beat you.

For my wedding I shall be dressed in red. I shall bring you my red gifts.

I threw my mother in the fire. I shall heal her. I shall heal her, with my tears.

My father and mother love each other so much. I came out of the fire between them. They marry inside me, in the red kitchen.

I take you inside me. I am not afraid of the fire any more. It is inside me. I am in the kitchen. You are there and you do not beat me.

Guillaume found he missed his daughter once she was married to Pierre and living down at the bottom of the hill in the schoolhouse. She did not come to Mass and so he never saw her in church. Sometimes on Sundays she walked along the village street with her husband, but she had little enough to say to her parents if she met them. Pierre kept a tight hold on her arm, and Guillaume did not know how to ask her the questions that longed to tumble out of his mouth. He thought perhaps the potato brandy had withered his tongue. The words burned his lips, then died. Sometimes Melusine climbed up the hill to visit her old home, but she sat by the fire in the kitchen gossiping to her stepmother and Guillaume was plainly in the way. Women's talk. He could not enter it, had never known how to. Sometimes he took her little gifts, a basket of eggs or a bunch of freshly picked rosemary or a calf's foot, and she would thank him with a nod and go back to her housework. The words he could not speak swelled in his throat and made it sore.

When Guillaume heard that Melusine was staying longer and longer each month in the pantry, he was persuaded by Madame Tarentin to go down and have a word with her. What word? He knew, but could not say it. She sat silent in front of his silence, and he went away again.

He drank at the bar less than he used to. He stayed at home with his wife and drank potato brandy in the kitchen, Madame Tarentin sitting close by him. They had begun to have a secret. Neither of them spoke of it to the other, but they read of it in each other's eyes. What was happening to Melusine? Would she go the same way as her mother?

On the night of the full moon in November of the year that Melusine disappeared, Guillaume crept out of his bed, down the hill and into the village. He stood underneath the schoolhouse pantry window and tapped at the closed shutters. No chink of light showed, but he knew his daughter was in there. His heart reached through all obstacles, knocking so loudly he knew Melusine must hear it.

She opened the windows, then the shutters, and leaned out in a swift glad movement, her eyes bright, a smile on her lips, her hands coming up in welcome. When she saw her father she drew back, all her delight falling off her like an old shawl.

—Oh, she said: it's you.

Guillaume reached up his hand and patted her arm. She frowned.

—Melusine, he pleaded, making an effort to get the words out of his burning mouth: please let me talk to you.

—Go away, she hissed.

She was dressed only in her nightgown. Tiny pleats flowed from the worn linen yoke. He reached his hands out and tore open the front of the nightgown, then clutched the folds of white linen so that she could not jerk back and escape from him. He saw the red skin, puckered and shiny and ridged, the scars as angry as though she had been dropped in the fire that very day.

—My daughter, he whispered.

Melusine shut her eyes, and turned her head away.

Then Guillaume wept. His tears fell on the scarred skin around his daughter's breasts and flowed onto his hands, warm and stinging. He could not see for weeping. So they remained at the window, the daughter and the father, knotted together by the nightgown, while Guillaume cried.

When he opened his eyes at last, he saw that the skin on his daughter's breast was as creamy and smooth as it had been on the day she was born, and that there was no blemish anywhere on her.

Footnote: I should like to acknowledge, with gratitude, the inspiration of the work of Toni Morrison.

COVETOUSNESS

ZOË FAIRBAIRNS

COVETOUSNESS

". . . culpable desire of possessing that . . . to which one has no right . . ."
Oxford English Dictionary

COVETOUSNESS

Suite 14, Tavistock House
Tavistock Mews
London WC1
January 14

My dear Maureen,
I have just put the phone down after talking to our New York
office and there is wonderful news: a very good offer indeed
for the US rights of *Blink and You'll Miss It.*

The offer comes from Ducades Inc., who, as you probably
know, are one of the biggest publishers of mass-market
paperbacks in the USA. They are not doing a lot of new British
fiction at the moment, but what they have done they have
done brilliantly successfully. They are confident that they can
do the same with *Blink and You'll Miss It* and their confidence
is reflected in the size of the advance that we have been able
to negotiate for you.

I'm delighted to be sending you this letter, and to be the
bearer of the news that your work is at last getting the financial
recognition it deserves.

Best wishes, and congratulations,
Yours sincerely,
Winifred.

37 Soweto Gardens
Stoke Newington, N16
January 15

Dear Winifred,
I am bewildered by your letter. I thought the US rights in *Blink and You'll Miss It* were being bought by those radical publishers in Connecticut. I know you didn't really approve of them but they were first! Can you please clarify?
    Thanks —
    Maureen.

Suite 14, Tavistock House
January 16

Dear Maureen,
Thank you for your letter. I will try to explain as best I can the situation as regards the Pallas Press of Connecticut.
    As you know, a year ago, following the British publication of *Blink and You'll Miss It,* they wrote to you saying that they thought it would fit well into their socialist-feminist fiction list. You passed their letter on to me and I sent it to our New York office.
    Not without difficulty, our New York office contacted the Pallas Press and endeavoured to pin them down as to their plans and intentions regarding the book. Certain verbal assurances were given, only to be contradicted by later verbal assurances. The Pallas Press appears to have rather a quick turnover of staff.
    Six months ago we gave them formal notice that if they did not make an offer in writing, we would consider negotiations to be at an end and offer the book elsewhere. We know that they received our letter, but answer came there none, so that is what has happened.

Shall I accept the Ducades offer? I don't want to rush you, but I don't think we should keep them waiting all that long for a decision.

> Best wishes,
> Winifred.

39 Soweto Gardens
January 16

Dear Maureen, Ros, Louise, Geoff and Toni,
Further to our conversation over supper, this is just to confirm that I am hoping to be able to put No. 37 on the market with vacant possession in June at the latest, so I'd be grateful if you could all start thinking about other arrangements. Sorry, but you know how it is.

> Love,
> Maggie.

37 Soweto Gardens
January 18

Dear Sir or Madam,
I am thinking of moving out of London, and your company has been recommended to me as specializing in country cottages in quiet areas within the commuter belt.

Would you please send me details of suitable properties currently on the market? I want either to bury myself in the country or gaze at the sea or both.

> Yours faithfully,
> Maureen Kent (Ms).

THE PALLAS PRESS
January 16

Dear Maureen,
Hi! I'm Stella and I'm the newest member of the Pallas Press
Collective. One of the reasons why I applied for the job was
that I was so excited to see *Blink* in the PP catalog.

I think you must be a very special person to have written
such a book. I want to thank you for writing it. It has
contributed to my growth as a woman and as a human being.
When your name came up in a discussion last night, I
volunteered to write to you.

A man in New York who says he is your agent is getting
heavy with us. He says he is taking *Blink* away from us and
giving it to Ducades. You probably don't know that Ducades is
one of the largest and most capitalistic publishing corporations
in the world. We're not surprised that they should want to
punish us by taking our books and our authors away from us,
but we can't believe that someone who could write a book
like *Blink* would go along with that.

We have already incurred production costs on the book and
we are hoping to have copies out in the bookstores very soon.

Is that man in New York really your agent? Please can you
ask him to stop this harassment?

Love and sisterhood,
Stella (for the Pallas Collective).

37 Soweto Gardens
January 23

Dear Stella,
I'm not sure about being a special person but I appreciated the
nice things you said about my book.

I'm sorry to hear about the trouble you've been having with

my agent's New York office. I don't know the man there at all.
He is saying that you don't have the US rights in *Blink and
You'll Miss It* because you never made any serious offer to buy
them.

Did he press you for an unrealistically large advance? I want
to know if he did.

You say you already have the book in production, so you
obviously believe that you have acquired the rights. Could you
send me the relevant correspondence?

In sisterhood,
Maureen
(Maureen Kent).

THE AGENTS GIVE NOTICE ON BEHALF OF THEMSELVES AND
THE VENDOR that although the following particulars have been
compiled in good faith they do not constitute an offer or contract
and are not to be relied upon as statements of fact. 5 Esplanade
Terrace, Leehaven, Sussex. A unique opportunity to acquire a
charming character property commanding magnificent views of
the English Channel and South Downs. This turn-of-the-century
coastguard cottage has been fully modernised to a high standard
by the present owner. Quiet location. Shopping centre and BR
3/4 mile away. Early inspection recommended.

THE PALLAS PRESS
February 1

Dear Maureen,
Whew! I'm glad you wrote, giving us the opportunity of
clearing up what could have become a source of discord

between us!

I'm enclosing a copy of the letter you sent saying that you wanted us to publish *Blink*. It's dated a year ago — we're under such pressure here that we can't always move as fast as the capitalist presses — so perhaps you forgot about it.

Advance orders are coming along well, especially from the women's bookstores!

Love,
Stella.

COPY

Dear Pallas Press,
Thank you for your letter. I was touched and delighted by your kind comments on my novel, and thrilled to know that you want to publish it in the USA. I have passed your letter to my agent who will be contacting you.

Best wishes, and thanks again,
Maureen Kent.

PS: By the way, the full title is *Blink and You'll Miss It*.

Suite 14, Tavistock House
February 9

Dear Maureen,
Thank you for your letter and enclosures.

To answer your question, no, I do not believe that what we have here is "an honest misunderstanding," I think what we have here is a very dishonest piece of what we literary agents call "trying it on."

Stella must indeed come from somewhere beyond the stars if she thinks that the words "I was thrilled to know that you want to publish it in the USA" constitute permission to produce a US edition of *Blink and You'll Miss It* without further correspondence, without a contract and without payment.

I must advise you to accept the Ducades offer and to do so promptly. They cannot be expected to wait for ever. Once the rights are theirs, I am sure we can rely on them to deal effectively with any attempt to produce a pirated edition.

    Yours sincerely,
    Winifred.

Kimberley Cottage, Seton Mulberry, St Mary Market, Kent. A deceptively spacious two-bedroom bungalow built one year ago and still under NHBC guarantee. Two reception rooms, garage, garden, panoramic views across Mulberry Valley. Central heating, double glazing, sun terrace. Wildlife park one mile distant. Owner emigrating, therefore realistic price for quick sale. It is the responsibility of any intending purchaser to satisfy himself by inspection or other means as to the truth or otherwise of any statement contained herein.

THE PALLAS PRESS
February 15

Dear Maureen,
Hi! I'm Carl, taking over from Stella who is in the hospital suffering from mononucleosis-related nervous exhaustion trauma (MRNET).

I am new to the collective, so let me say at the outset I am not personally responsible for any misunderstandings which may or may not have occurred in the past in connection with your novel *Blink*. This enables me to look at the current situation with objectivity. I believe that the Pallas Press has been to a large degree at fault. We have failed to explain to you the precise nature of our organization and its approach to working with authors.

We value personal contact with our authors very highly, and it is for this reason that we prefer not to use "contracts" or work through agents. Nor do we perpetuate the widespread mystification of authorship implied by paying advances. We believe that authors are an intrinsic part of the process whereby books are produced. Our usual arrangement therefore is that once overheads and production costs have been covered from sales of the book, we sit down with the author and discuss a profit share arrangement. This has always been very satisfactory.

Now that I have clarified the situation and accepted full responsibility for the part played by the Pallas Press in bringing about the present impasse, I look forward to receiving confirmation from you (or from your agent, if that is how you prefer to work with us) that you will not be selling out to Ducades, and that the US rights in *Blink* remain with us.

This confirmation will, I know, do more than medication can in restoring Stella to good health.

Love and comradeship,
Carl.

37 Soweto Gardens
March 20

Dear Mrs Hook,
I'm sorry if I sounded slightly wild on the phone. I had just taken delivery of a cheque for a rather larger sum of money than I had ever seen in my life, and you rang to ask whether I was available for a three-week assignment as a word-processor

operator at British Gas.

I hope you found someone else to do the job. Please take me off your books for the time being.

> Yours sincerely,
> Maureen Kent.

37 Soweto Gardens
March 20

Dear Mr Garston,
Please take this as notice that I no longer wish to be on your list of Casuals for the Friday evening shelf-filling shift.

> Yours sincerely,
> Maureen Kent.

37 Soweto Gardens
March 20

Dear Mr Lambert,
   Account No. 44522134A
From the contents and tone of your letter, I can only assume that you dictated it before your computers had registered the credit I paid in yesterday.

Your letters to me have become increasingly aggressive in recent months, and I am not prepared to tolerate your bullying for one moment longer. I am transferring my account elsewhere.

> Yours faithfully,
> Maureen Kent.

37 Soweto Gardens
April 3

Dear Mr Grimes-Hawthorn,
    Account No. 11098745L
Thank you for the delicious lunch. I can't think of a nicer
setting in which to hear about the wide range of financial
services offered by your bank.

As you said, we will have to agree to differ on the morality
of house-buying as a form of investment. I am not looking for
an investment, I am looking for a home. I have my eye on a
number of properties, and as the owner of the house which I
currently share with a group of friends is asking us to leave as
soon as possible, I expect to make my choice soon.

There is one other matter which is very petty and which I
am almost too embarrassed to raise. Every month (on the 5th)
my father transfers a small sum of money into my account.
Even before the recent improvement in my fortunes I asked
him to stop, but he would not. It is the Clothes Allowance that
he instituted when I was in my teens. I think he thinks he is
making an amusing point.

If any attempt is made to transfer this Standing Order to my
new account with you, would you please note that I do not
wish to receive any payment from this source.

    Yours sincerely,
    Maureen Kent.

AN URGENT MESSAGE TO FRIENDS OF RADICAL PUBLISHING
THROUGHOUT THE WORLD!
THE PALLAS PRESS OF CONNECTICUT FACES HUGE
PRINTING BILLS WHICH IT CANNOT PAY WITHOUT YOUR
HELP. CLOSURE MAY BE IMMINENT! PLEASE SEND
WHATEVER YOU CAN AFFORD. ALL CURRENCIES ACCEPTED.

17 River Walk
Twickenham
April 20

Dear Mo,

I'm doing a piece for the *Guardian* on radical novelists and I was all set to cite you as someone who hadn't sold out and never would. Then I heard this rumour that you took *Blink* away from Pallas because Ducades offered you more money.

Please, please tell me it's not true.

Love,
June.

Orchard Lodge
Oxby
Bucks
April 30

Dearest Maureen,

I laughed like a drain when someone showed me that thing about you in the *Guardian*. Reminded me of when you were a little girl. You were always a great one for being against things when you thought you couldn't have them, and changing your tune when you found you could.

Welcome to capitalism! It's warmer in than out, isn't it? I'm stopping your Clothes Allowance, by the way. I always said I'd go on paying it until you got yourself a proper job, a thing you seem now to have done with a vengeance.

What next? Any chance of you meeting a nice young man (or, on second thoughts, perhaps not so young) and discovering that you're not really "against" marriage either?

I'm only teasing. Take my advice. Swallow a bit more pride and get yourself some bricks and mortar. After forty years in the business I still say it's the best investment there is. Let me know when you've found somewhere you think you like and I'll survey it for you. I won't even charge you. Think of it as a lump sum payoff for your Clothes Allowance.

    Lots of love,
    Daddy.

PS: I'm kicking myself for donating the copy you gave me of "Blink and it's Gone" to the Lifeboats jumble. I couldn't get into it, but I imagine a signed first edition is going to be quite valuable one of these days. Don't sulk, you have to learn to take criticism if you're going to be a writer.

37 Soweto Gardens
May 2

To the Secretary
The Royal Institution of Chartered Surveyors

Dear Sir or Madam,
Would you please send me the names and addresses of Chartered Surveyors practising in this area.

    Yours sincerely,
    Maureen Kent.

37 Soweto Gardens
May 3

Dear Penny,
Thank you for your very sweet letter. Not everyone in the family has been so supportive.

I wish I could agree with you that any decision I make is bound to be the right one, but it was nice to have you say it. Want to hear about my next decision? I'm buying a house.

It's amazing, isn't it, that in spite of Daddy being what he is, I have managed to reach my late thirties holding steadfastly to the belief that home ownership has nothing to do with me. It isn't just that I've never had the money before. People poorer than I am — was — have bought flats.

It's a bit like sex, I think. When I was in my teens I was aware of it but I thought it was only indulged in by people older than me. By the time it dawned on me that people of my age and people younger than me participated and seemed to find it rewarding, I had decided that I did not want to and did not dare. Then all of a sudden one day I did want to and I did dare and I did.

I wish I hadn't started this analogy now, because what a farce *that* turned out to be, remember, I told you about it. I hope I'm not going to feel the same in fifteen years' time about owning Jessica Cottage.

Not that I own it yet. I've made an offer and it's been accepted. The present owner is an old lady with a hearing aid who wants to move into sheltered accommodation.

I have a sneaking feeling that she ran rings round me while we were negotiating. My heart wasn't in it. I was afraid of sounding like someone out of "Serious Money" and she seemed so vulnerable. I would have preferred it if the estate agent had been there, if only because Miss Burfleet was so deaf that we had to do everything in writing, but they sent me along on my own. What do these estate agents do to earn their commission?

Anyway, Miss B wouldn't budge very far on price but we haggled away about carpets and furniture, and I think I got a fairly good deal. Some of the furniture's lovely and it'll save me a lot of bother, having it in situ.

At this stage we're still subject to contract. Do you have

"subject to contract"? It means, "I may be lying."

Is it only in the property business that people precede every statement with the warning that you shouldn't believe a word of it?

Be that as it may, I wrote "subject to contract" on all my pieces of paper, at least I hope I did, I lost count rather.

Love to Ken and the children. When are you coming over again? Mo.

48 High Street
May 4

Dear Madam,
    Jessica Cottage
In accordance with your valued instruction, we have now inspected the above property and enclose our report thereon. If you require clarification of any of the points it contains, please do not hesitate to telephone us.
    Yours faithfully,
    HERIOT HENDERSON (Chartered Surveyors).

37 Soweto Gardens
May 7

Dear Miss Burfleet,
I am writing to let you know that I no longer wish to buy Jessica Cottage. My surveyor has drawn my attention to a number of points concerning its structure and condition of which I was not previously aware. He feels that the words "would suit DIY enthusiast or professional builder" would not come amiss when the property is readvertised.
    Yours sincerely,
    Maureen Kent.

21 Broad Street
May 9

Dear Madam,
    Jessica Cottage
We were surprised to receive, from the Vendor of the above property, a letter from your goodself stating that you no longer wish to purchase it.

We have in our possession other documents signed by you on the occasion of your inspection of the property. We are advised that, although of an informal nature, these constitute a legally enforceable contract to buy the property, at the agreed price.

The Vendor wishes to proceed with the sale, and we can only advise you to seek legal advice if you believe there has been any misunderstanding on this matter.
    Yours faithfully,
    HOLLAND, MURRAY, WALTERS
    (Estate Agents.)

Orchard Lodge
Oxby, Bucks
May 13

My dear Charles,
Cast your eyes to the signature at the foot of this letter and see if it rings the same bells for you as rang for me when I saw your name on your letterhead.

Are you the same Charles Holland I did my Articles with at Milton Bigglesmith Jones just after the war? Does the Blue Lagoon strike a chord? Francesca the barmaid? I say no more, old chap, it's not blackmail I have in mind after all these years, more of a favour. My daughter Maureen seems to have got herself into a bit of a mess with one of your branch offices, who seem to have used the one about the little old lady with the hearing aid to get her to agree to buy a shored-up ruin.

I'm not reproaching you, Charles. These are lean times. Frankly I blame myself. To have brought a daughter into the world who would forget to write "subject to contract"!

The temptation to leave her to stew in her own left-wing self-righteousness is enormous, but you know how it is. If I don't look after her, who else is going to? You must know what I'm asking, Charles.

The Blue Lagoon is now the Beefeater Tavern and heaven knows what's happened to Francesca, I imagine she'll have sagged a bit by now but then haven't we all? Let's meet there soon, I'm dying to catch up on all your news.

> Kind regards,
> Frank Kent.

21 Broad Street
May 14

Dear Frank,
I was delighted to hear from you after all these years, albeit distressed by the circumstances that led you to write.

Even in these competitive times, it is no part of company policy to harass or mislead inexperienced purchasers, whether or not they turn out to be the daughter of a friend of one of the partners. I have explained this firmly to the sales executive concerned, who has been given some clear advice as to future conduct.

In the meantime I am happy to confirm our understanding that Ms Maureen Kent's offer for Jessica Cottage was subject to contract and that she was entirely within her rights to withdraw the offer as she has done.

> Kind regards,
> Charles
> (Charles Holland, Holland Murray Walters.)

P.S. Is she Maureen Kent the writer? Francesca seems to think she must be. I don't read fiction myself, but Francesca's quite a fan. You must be very proud of her.

37 Soweto Gardens
May 17

Dear Maureen,
Your doctor said you weren't having any visitors for the time being but we hope the flowers arrived OK and that you'll soon be feeling better.

Maggie has been asking about you. She sends her apologies, she thinks the whole thing was her fault. She thinks she picked exactly the wrong moment to come round reminding us that she wants us all out of the house. You didn't injure her at all, she was just shaken, we all were, but you're being looked after now, that's the main thing.

Lots of Love,
Ros, Louise, Geoff, Toni.

Ward 6
May 19

Dear Maggie,
There is no point in saying I am sorry, after what I tried to do there can be no forgiveness so let us move on to matters practical i know you want vacant possession, unfortunately I am in no position to remove my belongings!!! please regard this letter as authorization to take everything out of my room and burn it i am sorry to be nuisance and for everything else, Maureen Kent.

Ward 6
May 20

Dear Maggie,
I have been thinking and I have had the most marvellous idea,
why don't I buy No 37 off you? Then when I come home from
hospital Geoff and Louise will be there not that I am going to
need looking after but it will be nice that they are there, and
Ros and Toni, we can all live there together for ever it will be
like old times, let me know how much you want for the house
Maggie and I will send you a cheque.
    Love,
    Maureen.

Ward 6
May 21

Dear Maggie,
I am wondering why you haven't responded to my offer to buy
your house, perhaps you are too busy dealing with surveyors
&c. The thing about surveyors, Maggie, is that they never say
anything nice, ever ever, they are paid not to, they would be
struck off the Surveyors' List if they did. My father never said
anything was good ever ever, he might say it was reasonably
satisfactory so far as he could ascertain, I went to a house with
him once, he was surveying it, I watched him prowling around
all slit-eyed and doom-filled as if he was about to punish
somebody, he measured and prodded and judged and I felt
sorry for the house. But the beauty of my idea, Maggie, is that
because we are friends, we won't have to bother with any of
that, we can just go ahead, let me know if you agree, this isn't
even Subject to Contract, I mean it, love,
Maureen.

Ward 6
May 25

Dear Maggie,
I think they are intercepting my post because I still haven't got
your answer please could you send a copy by special
messenger and tell him to speak to nobody but me I am in
Ward 6,
        Maureen.

Ward 6
May 26

Dear Maggie,
Perhaps the reason you are not answering is that you think I
am trying to cheat you, perhaps you think friendship should
not be a reason for not going through the proper channels, I
want you to know that I am not in the least bit offended that
you should want a banker's reference, I am writing to my bank
manager today to provide one,
        Maureen Kent.

39 Soweto Gardens
June 1

Dear Maureen,
I've been away for a few days and have come back to find your
letters, also the reference from your bank. It does seem that
you are in a position to buy yourself something nice, a cottage
in the country, perhaps, or a flat by the sea, but I'm afraid the
price I have to ask for No 37 puts it a bit out of your range.
    Louise and Geoff have finally found themselves a flat, and
they say to tell you that you're not to worry about your

belongings, they've got storage space in their roof and will keep everything safe until you're ready to collect it.

Ros and Toni have gone their separate ways. No 37 seems sad and empty without you all, I wish I hadn't had to do it but you know how it is. Get well soon, Maureen, and stay in touch.
    Love,
    Maggie.

Ward 6
June 2

Maggie:
You don't have to lie and be tactful. I know why you don't want to sell me your house, you think my money was illgotten, you don't want me under a roof that was once yours, you don't want anything to do with me, you don't think I have any right to spend all that money on myself, you don't think I earned it in the first place, you don't think I should have a home of my own, you think a person like me should always live in other people's,
    Maureen Kent.

Orchard Lodge
Oxby, Bucks
June 17

Dear Maureen,
What a time I've had tracking you down! Isn't that a loony-bin?

Are you having a nervous breakdown? What is a nervous breakdown? I mean, what form does it take? I've always wondered.

You're not really ill are you? Just a bit upset? Though God knows what you've got to be upset about. I mean, if you're upset what hope is there for the rest of us?

All this reminds me of when you were a little girl. You were always a great one for conveniently feeling ill to avoid the consequences of making a fool of yourself. You're not still worrying about that silly business with Jessica Cottage are you? I didn't mind helping you out. It gave me the biggest laugh I'd had for months to have you come to me like that, pleading for help. I'm dining out on the story but there's no malice in it, you know me.

Anyway you did me a favour putting me in touch with Charles Holland again; I hadn't seen him since just after the war.

Talking of whom, this will swell your head. His wife, Francesca, has heard of you! Charles says if you're still looking for a property and can bear to have anything further to do with his firm, ring him up and he'll look after you.

Don't buy anything, Maureen, without letting me look at it first. Not even from him. But do buy something and do it soon. The market waiteth for no man and property prices are ticking ever upwards while you sit in there weaving baskets or doing whatever you do. I could get some brochures off him and come and see you with them, would that cheer you up?

Lots of love,
Daddy.

14A Sydenham Mansions
SE 28
January 23

Dear Penny Marks,
You don't know us, but we are friends of your sister Maureen. We're writing to ask for your help. We know there's not much

you can do at this distance, but perhaps you can advise us at least.

We used to share a rented house with Maureen and some other friends. The house broke up while Maureen was in hospital and we agreed to keep her stuff in our flat. It's not a large flat, just two rooms, k & b and an attic, but we didn't mind doing that for Maureen.

Maureen came here when she discharged herself from hospital, we thought she would just stay long enough to get the paperwork done on a place of her own but that's not how it's turned out.

It's not that she's unwelcome, she's one of our best and oldest friends, she pays her way, we love having her, it's just that it's one thing having your roof full of your friend's bits and pieces, it's quite another to have her there, creeping about. We think she's got to make up her mind. If she's still ill and needs looking after, then she's got to be sensible and go back to her doctor. If she's okay, and she says she is, she's got to understand that she can't stay here for ever, frankly she is getting on our nerves.

To judge from our daily postal delivery she is on the mailing list of every estate agent in the country but nothing ever happens. Is there anything you can do, or suggest?

Yours sincerely,
Geoff Parkinson, Louise Burr.

473 Sunlight Drive
New South Wales 4023
January 30

Dear Geoff and Louise,
Does Maureen know that she is putting you under such strain? I know she is fond of you (sounds as if she damn well should be) but perhaps she doesn't realize. It sounds to me as if the

time has come for plain speaking, or at least stopping any pretence that things are OK.

Easier said than done I know, but it's all I can think of. I'll drop a line to our father too, he may be able to help her find a place, he's in the business.

Best wishes,
Penny.

Orchard Lodge
Oxby, Bucks
February 21

Dearest Maureen,
So that's where you're hiding!

There's no need to hide from me, old thing. If you don't want my help, say so. I've got better things to do, I can assure you, than house-hunt for someone who doesn't want to be house-hunted for.

If you think you can manage on your own, fine. I'm sure you can. People half your age buy and sell property with great aplomb these days. I'm sure you'll make a good choice, mistakes are part of the learning process, I'm sure you won't repeat the one you made over Jessica Cottage.

Do you realize that in terms of the way the property markets have been going your money is now worth only three quarters of what it was when you got it?

Lots of love,
Daddy.

16 Millwater Street
February 27

Dear Ms Kent,
    Account Nos 11098745L
          G11137
I wonder if you would be kind enough to call at the Bank at
your convenience for a short discussion on the conduct of
your account?

    There is of course more than enough money in your deposit
account to cover these large cheques which you have been
issuing in favour of various housing charities, and so the
cheques have been honoured. But it would simplify matters if,
in the future, you could remember to transfer the relevant
sums into your current account before issuing cheques.

    I would also like to point out that there are many more tax-
efficient ways of giving to charity than making large random
donations. I shall be happy to explain them to you.

    The Bank's customer leaflet on House Buying has just been
reprinted, so I am taking this opportunity of enclosing a copy
for your information.

    Yours sincerely,
    E. J. Grimes-Hawthorn, Branch Manager.

21 Broad Street
March 2

Dear Maureen,
Your father tells me that you have still not been suited so I am
enclosing particulars of one or two properties which may be of
interest to you.

My wife Francesca wants to know when there is going to be a sequel to *Blink and You'll Miss It*.
Kind regards,
Yours sincerely,
Charles
(Charles Holland.)

14A Sydenham Mansions
SE 28
March 3

Dear Charles,
Your wife Francesca is in good company, my American publishers and my British publishers and my agent and my agent's man in New York also want to know when there is going to be a sequel to *Blink and You'll Miss It* and so do I. When I have some peace and quiet and somewhere to sit down. If you think I can afford those properties you sent me you must be out of your mind, all my money is going, there is nothing I can do to stop it, it is just as well because I wasn't meant to have it in the first place. If you are out of your mind join the club. Please stop pestering me I am quite happy living with friends, yours,
Maureen Kent.

PROPERTY FOR SALE

MOVE TO A NEW TOWN! Many modern houses/flats available on estate convenient for M28. Bruce & Badley, Park St.

RECENTLY CONVERTED TO HIGH STANDARD. 2r k b g.c.h. Scope for DIY. Phone evenings.

STUDIO, quiet suburb. Suit first time or retirement.

CHARACTER PROPERTY with interesting features. Look no further.

The Haven
Camden Town
March 15

Dear Maureen,
Remember me from Ward 6? Next bed but two. How are you getting on? I am all right except I keep having things that remind me of other things. I saw an advertisement in the *Camden Free Paper*. It said, "ARE YOU OUT OF YOUR MIND? You'd have to be to buy this flat. Intrigued? sae for details to Box 5." It made me think of you. This is the sort of thing that keeps happening.
    Love from Gerry.

P.S. Have you written any more books?

14A Sydenham Mansions
March 16

Dear Sir or Madam,
Would you please send me details of the flat which you have
for sale and which I would be out of my mind to buy.
    Yours sincerely,
    Maureen Kent.

THE OWNER OF THE PROPERTY DESCRIBED BELOW
HEREBY GIVES NOTICE that all statements contained in these
particulars may be relied upon as factual.

Why would he make them up?

Any intending purchaser is at liberty to seek the advice of
any Surveyor, Solicitor, Mortgage Broker, Bank Manager,
Accountant or other paid professional pessimist, who will
advise against the purchase.

In the unlikely event of any person wishing to regard this
document as an offer or contract, he or she should feel free to
do so.

No 5 Rocky Heights, Lea Cliff, Sussex. Rocky Heights was
built as a country residence by a Victorian businessman in
1897. The soundness of its structure may be judged from the
fact that, having received the full force of gales from the
English Channel for nearly a century, it is still standing up,
albeit somewhat salty. It was converted into a hotel in 1953.

As such it was not a great success. Guests looking for
comfort after the hardships of war and rationing did not enjoy
the long climb through windswept downland, whispering
gorse and blackberry bushes. The lowing of cattle distracted
their attention from the speed at which real incomes were
rising. The changing moods of the sea — visible through most
windows and audible throughout the building — reminded
them of currents in the human soul. This was the last thing

they wanted to be bothered with on their summer holidays.

The building has recently been converted into flats. Some of the conversions have been more successful than others. No 5 has three huge rooms with bizarre ornate ceilings which may put you in touch with your Jungian archetypes and which are difficult to dust. Two of the fireplaces are useable, but as coal delivery trucks have difficulty getting up the track you may prefer to gather driftwood from the beach. The range in the kitchen is temperamental, like most good cooks. Sometimes your meal will be delicious, sometimes less so. You could rip out the range and replace it if you wished to do so. You could probably get a good price for it at one of those Original Features shops in South London.

The stains in the bath are not what they look like. Nothing shifts them.

The w.c. is new and does what it was put into the world to do.

There is no central heating.

The gutters need to be replaced but they probably won't be.

The chimney stacks have defied the laws of gravity for some years and there is no special reason to suppose they will not continue to do so.

With a bit of effort most windows can be persuaded to open and close.

Let me know what time your train gets in and I will pick you up.

MARCUS MERILEES.

16 Millwater Street
March 20

Dear Ms Kent,
    5 Rocky Heights
As you requested, I have shown the particulars of the above
property to one of our Personal Advisers on First Time
Purchases. Without having seen the property, all she can advise
is that you proceed, if at all, with extreme caution, a view
which I wholeheartedly endorse.

    Mr Merilees is of course entitled to his view of me, my
colleagues and others in related professions. May I, in my
capacity as paid pessimist, suggest that you take a companion
with you if you decide to inspect his property?
    Yours sincerely,
    E. J. Grimes-Hawthorn, Branch Manager.

Rocky Heights
March 30

Maureen my darling —
Two days have gone by since you were here, and still I am
dazed, ecstatic, bewildered. How did it happen? I don't do this
kind of thing. But the moment you got off the train I knew.
And you knew too — didn't you? Tell me it was real. Tell me it
truly happened and that you are glad. Come again and I will
show you the rest of the flat.
    Endless, endless love,
    Marcus.

473 Sunlight Drive
New South Wales 4023
March 30

Dear Louise, dear Geoff —
I was sorry to hear that your gentle hints to Maureen have
fallen on stony ground and that she is still in situ. I do think
that the time has come to be cruel to be kind. You say she
"wanders off to look at properties" from time to time but it
never goes any further . . . next time perhaps you must force
the issue by simply locking her out of the house. After all,
she's not a pauper; she'll find somewhere to go.
    Let me know what happens —
    Best wishes,
    Penny.

14A Sydenham Mansions
SE 28
March 31

Dear Marcus,
Yes it was real, and yes I'm glad, and no I don't do that kind of
thing either, and yes I want to see you again but I'll have to
forget about buying your flat, I mean one has to be
hardheaded about these things, I suppose I should sign this
letter "subject to contract" — oh dear do I want you again.
    Love,
    Maureen.

Rocky Heights
April 2

Dear Maureen,
Yes, by all means be hardheaded. How clever of you to see
through my trickery. What happened between us was simply

my way of distracting your attention from what an unwise thing you would be doing if you were to buy Flat 5.

Its many advantages as a place to live in pale into insignificance against the single awful truth: IT IS A LOUSY INVESTMENT. The reason for this is to do with the design of the building. Flat 5 is not, and cannot be made, self-contained. Whoever buys it will have to share a staircase (the rather lovely cast-iron spiral one, did you notice) with me.

Not such a terrible fate, one might think, given the low asking price and the general beauty of the place. But no one grants mortgages on non-self-contained properties, so it would always be difficult to resell.

Potential purchasers are restricted to peculiar people with cash.

5 Rocky Heights is a home, pure and simple.

But not yours, I think.

As a favour to me, have a surveyor look over the place and confirm that everything I have said is true. Choose your own surveyor, send the bill to

> Your grieving and misunderstood
> Marcus.

> 14A Sydenham Mansions
> SE 28
> April 3

Dearest Marcus

Please forgive me, I didn't mean to hurt you, I am afraid I may be a chartered surveyor at heart.

> Love,
> Maureen.

Rocky Heights
April 4

Dear Maureen,
Forgiven. Why don't you come for the weekend. I'll keep all
pens out of sight and then you won't be tempted to sign
anything. We'll be too busy. I want to kiss you all over your
body. The thought of you drives me wild with love and desire.
It is for you to satisfy yourself by inspection or other means as
to the truth or otherwise of the foregoing statements, we can
go for walks as well. I bought *Blink and You'll Miss It* from
Smith's. I told the woman I knew you. Not knew you, just
knew you. She said to ask whether there's going to be another
book soon. Your loving
    Marcus.

14A Sydenham Mansions
SE 28
April 9

Dear Penny,
Further to your recent advice, you may like to know what has
happened. Maureen is away for the weekend, god knows
where, and I said to Geoff, fine, now's our chance, she's out,
she can stay out. And I started packing up her stuff. Geoff said,
oh we can't. I said, oh we can. It developed into a major row,
all the tensions of the past few months coming out and now
Geoff has left.

   I'm not blaming you, Penny. But I thought you might
appreciate the irony.
    Louise.

14A Sydenham Mansions
SE 28
April 10

Dearest Marcus,
Thank you for the beautiful weekend. But I've come home to
some terrible news. My flat mates have split up. I feel
responsible and I can't walk out on Louise in her time of need.
I'm going to have to stay here, she's in a dreadful state.
    Love,
    Maureen.

Rocky Heights
April 12

Whatever you say, my dear Maureen. But if disappointed
Vendors and indecisive Purchasers are to last very long as
lovers, there must be no shred of suspicion between them.
    Please take me up on my earlier offer. Have a surveyor look
over Flat 5 and confirm the truth of everything I have said
about it.
    My love is also true.
    Marcus.

48 High Street
April 20

Dear Madam,
    Flat 5 Rocky Heights
In accordance with your valued instruction, we have now
inspected the above property.
    Our detailed report is enclosed herewith. In summary we
would say that, although, having regard to the age and position

of the property, its general condition appears, subject to the exclusions outlined in the report, to be, so far as we can ascertain, reasonably satisfactory, and although the asking price is considerably lower than that for three-room flats elsewhere in the area, resale would be extremely difficult and we cannot therefore recommend the purchase.

Assuring you of our best attention at all times.

Yours faithfully,

HERIOT HENDERSON (Chartered Surveyors).

14A Sydenham Mansions
SE 28
April 23

Dear Heriot Henderson Chartered Surveyors,

Why don't you people mind your own bloody business? It's my money and I'll do what I want with it.

What a joyless bunch you are, never buying anything until you're sure you'll be able to get rid of it.

When you were little, didn't your mothers ever tell you, "If you can't think of anything nice to say, don't say anything at all"?

I don't suppose you ever were little, come to think of it.

Yours in disgust,

Maureen Kent.

473 Sunlight Drive
NSW 4023
September 4

Dear Maureen,

Thanks for making our visit such a lovely one. It was too short, as these trips always are, and now we're back, jetlagged and exhausted and asking ourselves where all the time went.

The girls are ecstatic about your amazing flat and I am ecstatic about your man. It seems a good arrangement for people like the two of you: separate flats, shared staircase. I wouldn't mind something like that myself sometimes.

Ken has just read the last sentence over my shoulder and he says that he wouldn't mind either. He says he can think of quite a few couples who wouldn't mind. He says that in view of the obvious trend towards separate-togetherness among couples, you've probably got a fairly valuable property there.

I hope all is going well with the new book. Now I have a request to make on behalf of Claire. She was so impressed with you that she has decided to "do" you for Show and Tell. She is going to hold up a copy of *Blink and You'll Miss It* and tell her friends about her clever English aunt. She has dictated some questions, for which I take no responsibility, I am just the typist.

CLAIRE'S QUESTIONS.

1. Are you rich?
2. Have you ever met the Queen?
3. Why do you live in that funny house?
4. How do you get ideas for stories?
    Lots of love,
    Penny.

                                            Flat 5
                                            Rocky Heights
                                            September 20

Dear Claire,
I have never met the Queen.
    Lots of love,
    Maureen.

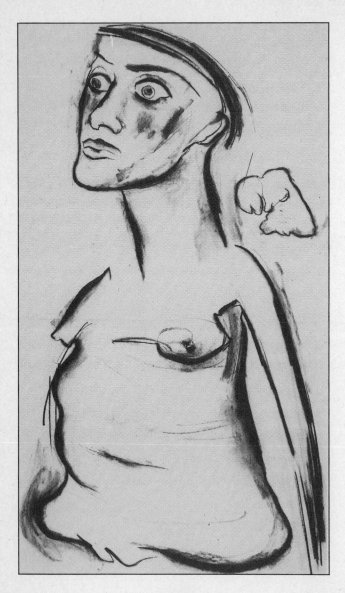

SLOTH

ALISON FELL

SLOTH

"Sister Whale"

"I am sloth. I was begotten on a sunny bank, where I have lain ever since, and you have done me great injury to bring me from thence. Let me be carried thither again by Gluttony and Lechery. I'll not speak another word for a king's ransom."

Christopher Marlowe, *The Tragical History of Doctor Faustus*

SLOTH

THE FIRST THING THE TRAVELLER LEARNS IS THAT SHE DOES NOT EXIST

It's autumn at the end of the world. On a packed Easter plane heading south, Dee flicks through the *Sydney Morning Herald*. The belly of the plane is ribbed and pale and bucks occasionally in the turbulence of the Bass Strait. Down below is a deep green sea, white specks which could be waves or sails, and the blue strip of coastal shallows tapering west to Melbourne.

She skims an article on Japanese tourism, restless, critical. As far as she's concerned the paper is full of omissions. For instance, only ten days since Reagan's planes bombed Tripoli but not a word about Libya. A wingeing Pom they'd call her in Sydney, where the earth spins on a different axis and certain conversations are impossible. Conversations about Europe, that lovely dead leaf she lives on. Conversations that tell you who you are.

"Yay well," Mona had drawled down the phone, "bunch of provincials, your Aussies. World ends at bloody Bali, didn't you know." Insisting then that Dee fly down for Easter instead of waiting until May, when her writing Fellowship ended. "Never mind the money, I want my little sister back." Her laugh had quivered with the effort of asking, and Dee had said of course she'd come, of course, knowing suddenly and uneasily that she shouldn't have waited to be persuaded. It had been nineteen, twenty years, after all. Since they met.

The plane banks, setting its course. Directly below, everything is dizzyingly water. Shutting her eyes, Dee holds on to her stomach, holds it in.

Mona looms now, shadowy, placid: Mona the loyal sister, the biddable daughter. Mona whose husband left her five years ago: just upped and offed with a married woman.

If Mona's devotion had always been quiet and complete, so, it seemed, was her breakdown. Her dutiful letters faltered and stopped, were replaced by the sort of cheery gut-gripping bulletins their mother resorted to in times of crisis. *Mona is seeing a nice psychiatrist weekly, she is managing better now thanks to the pills . . .*

When Mona's letters resumed they were changed, harsher. She was reading Germaine Greer — *I expect you read her years ago, I guess I'm just a late developer;* she seemed to be seeing things differently. From London Dee sent out books, pamphlets, addresses of women's groups in Melbourne and Sydney. Privately she thought that the break-up might be for the best.

The plane levels and steadies, and the sea settles back. Dee shakes her head. Twenty years, though. *Twenty years and hundreds of thousands of words and not one of them about Mona.*

I Don't Remember Mona Being There.

Childhood: a time of snow. One night near Christmas, Dee asked to go with her father to steal a tree from the Forestry Commission. Black firs, white forest floor: the memory sharp-edged, irresistible.

The spade they'd brought was redundant. The ground was frozen far too hard to dig. Her father placed her hands on the bowed handle of the saw and wrapped his warm fingers around hers, showing her the ropes. In magic moments like this there are no other women, sister, mother, grandmother. Protective amnesia. She defines herself as the only child, special, necessary.

She stuffs the errant newspaper back in the rack. Her hands are sweating. She and Mona had been too close, always. Mona was impossible to stand back from, impossible to define.

Down below the island begins, brown, tree-dotted, swathed with mist and rainbows. In her mind's eye Mona swells, is without beginning, middle or end.

THE THIN GIRL AND THE FAT GIRL

Once upon a time there was a thin girl who thought every morsel she put into her mouth would turn her into a whale.

If she had lived in Victorian times she might have welcomed the tyrannies of whalebone, which would have given her willpower a rest.

However, she lived in the permissive eighties, which was quite a problem.

Every day she either exercised or worried about not exercising.

Every day she either ate salad or worried about not eating salad.

Every day she wrote, and worried about the next day, when she might be blocked.

One day, puffing along the river bank on her morning run, she came upon a water snake, long and slim and muscular as a narrative.

"What do you think will happen, thin girl," the snake asked, "if you stop trying to keep yourself in?"

"I'll blow up like a balloon, of course," the thin girl replied crossly. "It's all very well for you, thinness is your very nature."

"Balloons can float," the snake persisted. "Why don't you give it a go?"

"Balloons can burst," the thin girl argued, "and then there'd be nothing left, would there? No author, no story . . ."

"Then you're back in your cleft stick, aren't you," the snake retorted, and, turning tail, he slithered down the bank towards the shady water. But he was a handsome snake, diamond-patterned and very sleek, and the thin girl wasn't ready to relinquish him just yet.

"Hang on a minute," she said prettily, "and ask me one more question if you'd be so kind."

"No worries, mate," the snake replied, and repeated the question somewhat grumpily. "What do you think will happen, thin girl, if you stop keeping yourself thin?"

This time the thin girl thought hard. "I'll swallow a huge suet pudding," she said triumphantly, "and be constipated for a hundred years!"

The snake sighed heavily. "Can't you tell the difference between good and bad things to eat by now?" he said, and producing a crisp autumn apple, he held it out towards her.

"Can't you see I'm too hungry to discriminate?" the thin girl shouted, and, snatching the apple, she rammed it so hard into the poor snake's jaws that he rolled helplessly down the bank and disappeared without trace under the shady surface of the water.

Once upon a time there was a fat girl who thought she would surely faint if she didn't peck at some morsel every half hour.

If she had lived in Suffragist times she might have welcomed force-feeding, for then she wouldn't have had to swallow her anger as well.

However, she lived in the enfranchized eighties, and had freedoms like everyone else.

Every day she built anxious barricades of Smartie packets around her typist's desk, and in the glove compartment of her car stored secret Mars Bars in case of traffic jams.

One evening, eating Pavlova cake on her balcony, she saw a bright blue parrot on a wattle branch above her.

"What do you think will happen, fat girl," asked the parrot, flying down to perch on the balcony rail, "if you stop keeping yourself so fat?"

The fat girl eyed him nervously. "Well, you will knock me down with a feather," she replied.

"And if I had no intention of knocking you down?" asked the blue parrot amiably.

"Then you will peck at me and hurt me," said the fat girl, wrapping plump arms around herself for protection.

"And if I only wanted to snuggle up?" asked the parrot, fluttering down onto the arm of her deckchair.

The fat girl jumped up, afraid. "Can't you see I'm too fat to snuggle up to?" she cried angrily. And without another word she snatched up the parrot, strangled him, and ate him up feathers and all.

I am not Jack Kerouac

And now there is Hobart, they are coming in low over Storm Bay, chinning the waves, wing-wobbling like a black bat. Down below, seaweed inlets, a windsock cocking the finger. Somewhere in the back of her beyond, Bahrain is a flat sand-dump of minarets, Singapore a bad skid, electric rain, and all the things she ever wanted to do or be jam into the bottom of her stomach as the wheels touch down oh so lightly and the jet thrust reverses to churn the air and then cuts to a whine as they come to the sweetest of hundred yard stops and taxi to a low building not so much bigger than a boy-scout hut where her long-lost sister, her big sister, her unfamiliarly big sister, stands nineteen years later in a middle-age tent dress with a pale hand raised. Waving. Silvered lovely long nails and tears in her eyes she looks embarrassed about.

"Oh you skinny wee thing!" Mona gasps, after Dee races across the tarmac wondering what age Mona will read in her gaunter face; it feels like embracing a warm wide immovable tree bole with some give in it, a soft cedar maybe (something she has always associated with Mona's red hair which is faded now and wears regular oblong streaks of blonde) and she has raced across the tarmac worrying needlessly for there in Mona's eyes she sees herself as she always was: the not-Mona, the boy-one, the wee one, the thin frenetic one, the one Mona used to push over with her little finger, rallying her weight behind it and Dee went down giggling and grateful because it was a relief sometimes to meet a Mona who resisted, a Mona who could win . . .

Mona had soft blue-veined breasts in the bath and I shuddered. Dee wails: "Not a line on your face, God, look at me, how do you do it?"

Flushing with pleasure, Mona releases her. "You're leaner, that's why. Don't knock it!" She wears a brown crocheted shawl over her shoulders; a Polynesian-looking necklace of large wooden beads lies on the shelf of her breasts.

Dee knows from photographs what to expect but not the effect it will have on her. This size that Mother warned her not to comment on, these breasts which keep her dourly at a distance. She keeps talking instead of crying as Mona moves regally towards the exit with her handbag over her arm, Mona who took the £10 passage just before the sixties kissed their generation with all its promises, Mona whom she hadn't quite forgiven for not sharing in any of it, maybe not even caring, and settling instead for a house with a view and a taut man who required his egg and bacon early . . .

The car passes blue gums and fields of button-grass glittering in a sun even harsher than Sydney's.

"Yay well," says Mona in her odd new accent, "there's a band of atmosphere that lets the ultra-violet through. You have to watch out for our sun in Tassie." Mona the Australian citizen. In whose country Dee is only temporary, a tourist.

Mona's body doesn't turn when she speaks, her breasts don't move. Her head is stately and immobile. Only her hand makes an occasional slow arc to tap ash into the ashtray or lift a small bottle of orange squash to her lips, a bottle with a straw in the top. Beside the bottle, in a compartment between the seats, there are cigarettes, a lighter, a half-pound bar of chocolate.

Mona is talking about whales, rainforests, conservation. But what about her weight, her heart? Her heart with all that weight, her blood pressure at the very least? Near tears, Dee nods politely. Well, who wouldn't worry about their heart? She certainly does. Particularly when she's been smoking and writing for hours tensely and her right arm cramps from wrist to elbow; look what happened to their father, a coronary at fifty-six so Mona can't pretend it isn't in the family, can she?

Mona sips squash through the straw, delicately, a stranger. In profile, though, the bones still show: a straight nose, domed brow, strong chin. Dee stares at a small unspoiled ear. Hands across her stomach, holding herself in. She must have it out with Mona, talk, yes, ask her if she ever imagines those first signs. Constricting arteries, thrombosis.

Words:

How many? A vocabulary of what? 2,000? Maybe 3,000? In Sydney the students pour them at her: narratives, subtexts; the students pour into her office, students of all nationalities, students shy as possums, students who offer cigarettes and words. Perhaps if she stopped trying to write, if she stopped trying, she might see images, might see. An explosion, an exploding author: Sadeian words, the sphincter released. The original bodylove of pleasure, sucking, shitting.

She ought to breathe deeply. In, out. Someone ought to tell her that despair is a constriction against devils, bodyhate of blood, of girlhood, wrapped tight and narrow around her.

They are coming over a long curving hill when Mona shoulders the car off the road and up a sudden steep driveway. And there is the house, ranch-style, set on a slope and hedged in on all sides by thick underbrush.

"Big," Dee says, and big it is. Apart from which, nothing is as she expected. On the veranda wattle trees weep brown leaves she itches to sweep up. Inside, empty squash bottles march mournfully across the corners of the kitchen, and dead hydrangea heads butt at the livingroom windows. She stands with her rucksack on her back, shocked somehow, making allowances.

Christ, it's not as if she's domestic herself. Think of the men who've made a point of telling her so, who've tried to tidy her up, to wipe round her bathtub and scour out her teacups and unravel the cords of her blinds. But you're either your father's daughter or your mother's daughter. And wasn't she always *supposed* to be the bohemian? And wasn't Mona supposed to be the home-maker?

In the spare room where she throws her rucksack the sag of the mattress has been bolstered with an ill-fitting strip of foam rubber. Even the wide-windowed livingroom looked dusty and exhausted, as if the owner had long been absent.

She splashes water on her face and goes back through to Mona. Poor thing, she thinks. Poor Mona. Pinching the place between her eyebrows where temper and tension lodge.

The Uses of Clothespegs:

The hole in the end of a clothespeg was just big enough to hold her little finger yet small enough to slightly and satisfactorily pinch it.

You could also nip your nose with it, or your earlobe or the pad of flesh below your thumb and when you flapped your hand the clothespeg would stay there hanging on by its pincers like a crab. Also on the edge of the palm which didn't actually hurt but pinched firmly nonetheless. She has seen little girls put clothespegs up them and apple cores and the like but never nip their vaginal lips together although why should she suddenly think of that is quite beyond her.

Chalk and Cheese

"I got you the typewriter," Mona says eagerly. "Did you see the typewriter?"

It's silly to think of working, really, since she's due back in Sydney on Tuesday and there's nothing in the house that would serve as a desk, but Dee thanks her anyway. *See and have a good rest*, Mother had urged on the telephone, frail mother, fretting. *Mona knows how to take it easy but you will overdo it, won't you.* Two daughters, and how different they are. But what about the housecoat Mona has changed into? A housecoat flowered in brown and orange, awful, colours she has always hated. And what about the dress mother sent her last Christmas, that long brown shapeless evening dress. Hopeless. *Something nice for your poetry readings*, the card said. The nylon gave her small electric shocks. She held it up in front of friends, marvelling, donated it to Oxfam, and went on puzzling. Until now, that is. Now it's eerily clear that Mother couldn't tell one daughter from the other; Mother simply got her daughters mixed up.

She absolutely must not laugh wildly, explode: it's too painful, funny, no it's not, Mona will never see the joke.

Differentiation

Mona fills two glasses with Glenfiddich and they sit down on two facing fawn settees, Mona squarely, Dee astride an arm. Fidgeting in the face of Mona's great stillness, Dee raises her glass, toasts in Gaelic: *"Sláinte."* Ironic for the old country.

Mona reaches for a cigarette. Exactly at her elbow an ashtray on a chrome stalk overflows with butts. Dee smiles. *Housekeeping, God no, I'm no great shakes in that department.*

"Bit of a slob, right," Mona grins, relaxing back into the sofa. "When Gary was around, well . . ." Her shrug indicates what a relief it was to give up the effort. She kicks off her shoes, and tucking her feet up on the sofa, smiles heavily. "Life can really deal them, eh?"

Dee nods, edgy. Poor thing. Poor Mona. She rocks on the sofa arm, scissoring her knees. Poised for the confessions to come. But after all this time it's much too soon, somehow. For Gary. For Mona's pain, so big and thick and only to be guessed at.

Under her housecoat Mona is wearing pop-socks not tights; her bare broad knees are girlish and dimpled. Dee tries not to stare. In her narrow black pants she is Billy the kid again, is the Lone Ranger — every lean tough fast male role Mona ever surrendered to her.

And Mona says: "Sounds like you didn't have too much luck with your last bloke, either."

Dee looks sharply out of the window and further. Beyond the glass the dead-heads nod stupid and heavy as love or jet-lag or any of the other things she doesn't want to talk about. Or at least not yet, not now, not after twenty years, not to Mona.

On the other side of the garden hedge a long hill slopes down past contained outbreaks of bungalows to a blue harbour, the arc of the Tasman Bridge, supply ships nosing south towards Antarctica. Mona points to the far hazy side of the bay. "A school of whales got stranded there last summer, poor things. Their sonar goes wrong, they get beached."

"Don't they die just from gravity or something?"

"Yay. You've got to get them back into the sea." Mona's eyes swim briefly in a sheen of tears. "Their own weight can crush them to death."

Briefly in the garden some kind of parrot squawks. Mona always was too tender-hearted. Couldn't kill a fly, Mother used to say. Dee laces her fingers together and looks down at them. "Remind me to prune your hydrangeas," she says.

Mona's eyebrows, which she still pencils a sharp dark sixties' brown, shoot up and sit startled and without jollity in her wide pale face.

"Be my guest!"

"Oh, you know me." Dee flashes a wide grin. "Always have to be on the go."

"Yay well." And now Mona really does smile. Her round eyes drink Dee in and in. One silver nail sits sweet in a dimple. Under the flowered housecoat her shoulders are shaking.

She's laughing, she says, at Dee's teeth, which are large and good and gapped.

Obligingly, Dee snaps them together. All the better to eat you with.

"I've got a bloody bridge, me. Comes out at night."

Dee giggles, horrified. "No kidding?"

"Twenty years," Mona groans. "Jesus we're middle-aged."

A Woman's Right to be Lazy

Memories spill.

"The cold, God save us, remember the cold?"

Sheets frozen like boards on the washing line, not to mention Granny's pink knickers, those relics with their all-too-human folds

*flattened by permafrost. Sleety afternoons shivering up the street
from school, the bronchitic chill of the Kirk and the hymnbooks
dank in their dark red covers . . .*

Mona's hand dips dreaming into an open bag of Smarties. "What *I*
remember" — face alight with excitement and guilt — "is that
you could never just DO NOTHING."

They make a list. They laugh dreadfully. It's exhausting just
thinking about it.

*Thinking of Granny always on the go, flouncing feather dusters
round the livingroom, blacking the grate, brassoing the candle-
sticks, chopping furious kindling in the woodshed, rolling out the
pastry, tying up the blackcurrant bushes, raking dead birds and
leaves from the gutters, darning the winter socks, scrubbing coal
dust and flour from under her fingernails daily, bottom lip
between her teeth, scowling down at the hard-bristled nailbrush.*

"What about Mother, though — Never idle!"

"Except when she smoked. Her excuse. 'Must have my fag.' "

Simultaneously, they bring out cigarettes, flare their lighters.
Remembering Mother at 7 am in a quilted housecoat, hurrying,
two curlers tangled forgotten in her hair and her dreams tucked
into the corners of her mouth. There was toast to make and eggs
to scramble and fresh rolls, maybe, to fetch from the baker's, and
father's temper, too, testy at that time of day. *Steamheels, he called
her, for she never walked but ran, flustered, on short eager legs
like a small pony, ran to get the rolls or sew on the button or iron
the blouse or retrieve the clean overalls.*

The wood stove has been lit, the whisky bottle sits on the floor
between them. Mona looks at Dee, and Dee looks at Mona: check
and double-check. Was it like that, God, was it really? They giggle,
leading each other on, collaborating. Dee shrieks and tugs at her
hair. Mona's eyes glow. With her stockinged foot she pushes the

bag of Smarties towards Dee. "Just help yourself, you know?"

Dee eats them one by one and is happy. Too happy, even: her skin feels too thin to hold it. The fire flickers, and the feeling swells in her. Mona's eyes never leave her. And for a second it's almost frightening, to realize just how badly she has wanted her big sister back.

High Standards

A spasm of pain crosses Mona's face. "Repeated Stress Injury. Lots of the girls get it." She massages her arm from wrist to elbow. "Bloody eggheads expect their reports done yesterday."

At the Research Division Mona types fomulae onto a fluorescent green screen: formulae predicting the rates of growth of certain tree moulds, algae, crop-threatening aphids. Stressful? Yes it's stressful, always being the dogsbody. Barbara keeps telling her she could do better.

"Cut loose, train as a counsellor maybe." She looks shyly at Dee. "People say I've got that sort of, you know, sonar?"

Dee is nodding hard. Sounds terrific. Just the thing.

On the mantelpiece there's a collection of owls: ceramic owls, wooden owls, owls with smiles, owls made from pine cones and cut glass and iron pyrite. Mona passes her hand over them, touches them diffidently, as if they're people she's afraid to intrude on.

"You could go to college." Dee grasps a granite owl forthrightly and massages it in a muscular palm. "I don't know why you never went to college."

Mona freezes. "Aim higher, eh?" She shakes her head infinitesimally; it's as if she only shakes her eyes.

"Lots of women start late nowadays."

Mona looks down at the owls, flushing. "Fear", she says finally.

"The psychiatrist said he saw fear."

"Fear Christ yes well no wonder . . ." Dee hurries, and it's true, there's every excuse (but me too Mona I am terrified of my shadow), just take a look at their childhood and what they weren't allowed to do:

As far as she remembers
Touch ourselves (either nipping or not nipping the vaginal lips together but they've never discussed any of this). Compete. Be jealous. Lie. Complain. Be ungrateful. Be greedy. Be pushy. Be independent/dependent. Explore. Despair. Show off. Be shy. Quarrel. Retreat. Reflect. Chatter. Flirt. Be tomboyish. Brood. Laze. Be mad, be bad, be plain, be vain.

Fear Christ yes no wonder. The very thought makes a perverse magic. She takes a deep breath. Imagine loving and hating. Imagine your good big teeth taking a good big bite out of Mona.

Opportunities

Mona opens the door of the stove to put more logs on. The red heat glows out.

And Dee says: "What I remember is . . . what I remember is there was NO PLEASING ANYBODY." She stretches out on the rug and yawns hugely; the room swims in her watering eyes.

"You must be worn out," Mona says sympathetically, "what with the book and the job and everything."

Dee nods, basking, the whisky biting warmly. *Anybody but Mona, that is.* She could always rely on Mona, couldn't she. To be her best ear, her very best audience. That's the awful thing.

"Maybe it's not the best moment to say so, but Tess Gilchrist rang from the Writers' Union. To ask you to lunch."

"Lunch?" Dee echoes, reluctant.

"I think they want to set up a reading or something." Mona's smile is merry and wry. "I'm getting to feel quite a celebrity around here, with such a famous sister."

Dee clutches her forehead, allows herself a groan. Now there's self-indulgence for you. Craving the limelight, but when it comes to it she'll tie herself in knots — You always were backward about pushing yourself forward, Mother says — when it comes to it her shoulders will lock and her smile congeal as she chokes her way through vegetable flan and apricot mousse, *all from our own garden*, the host will say nervously, nicely . . . unable to taste a thing, she'll say the word Wonderful far too often, that silly hollow sound of shyness, such a giveaway, it's enough to bring her out in a cold sweat just thinking about it. . .

The surprise on Mona's face stops her short. "But honestly, if you don't feel like it. I mean, Tess seems okay. I'm sure she wouldn't mind if . . ."

Dee has a terrible urge to cry. Let me make you some pancakes, she hears Mother say, have a currant scone, one slice or two? Yes, full, warm, protected, the promise little girls get. Yes, she'd rather stay right here with Mona and never say another word. But be careful crossing the road, mind out for the snow, the sun, the ants, the darkness; that's the other side of it, the glue that sticks you.

She shakes her head. Overtired. She must be overtired. Someone is being babyish here. And she hasn't got this far by coddling her phobias, has she? "No really. Fine. I'll call her."

"Well, as long as you feel up to it," Mona says doubtfully.

THE DEVIL'S DILEMMA

The Devil's sexual appetites being common knowledge, it came to pass that in the course of his several marriages seven children were born. Much to the Devil's chagrin, every last one of them was a daughter, and having little patience with girls or their names, he simply called each one after whatever sin happened to take his fancy at the time of her birth.

Being the last of seven, the youngest daughter was an awful bother to her exhausted mother, who had married the Devil late in life with the intention of either wheedling from him a recipe for eternal youth or at the very least enjoying a leisured old age in the bosom of his riches. The Devil, however, was tight with his elixirs, and what's more, expected value for money.

One day, finding his wife cleaning the kitchen floor with a Squeezy mop like anyone else, he became extremely angry.

"That's all very well for the au pair," he said, and he snatched the mop away and led the poor woman by the ear to the broom cupboard, where the scrubbing brush was. "But as for you, madam, you'll get down on your knees and do the thing properly."

Meanwhile the youngest daughter toddled along behind, making wet sympathetic sandalprints on the cork tiles and driving her mother to distraction. While her mother scrubbed, the girl did her best to be helpful, screwing fallen fluff and hair combings into little balls and drying the floor with the hem of her dress. But all to no avail, for her mother was impatient to get back to her elixirs, and huffily pushed her daughter away.

After several aeons of this, the youngest daughter lost heart with helpfulness, and trotted off to see if she could be her father's favourite instead.

Since her sisters — apart from Envy, who wore boys' clothes and wasn't someone you'd wish for an enemy — were indistinguishably dowdy and uniform, she put on a bright red dress in order to be special and toured Hell until she came to the great Ballroom. Here she found the Devil relaxing in front of the football results, his feet up on a pouffe and his belly luxuriant under his favourite knitted waistcoat.

The youngest daughter waited and watched for an opportunity to show her mettle. When finally her father snapped his fingers and cried out for his ashtray, she raced to fetch it before any of her sisters. But in doing so she collided first with Envy, who pinched her nastily for her trouble, and then with Anger and Covetousness, who were also hanging around waiting to curry favour, and fell right into the coal scuttle, dirtying her red dress abominably.

Displeased by the delay, the Devil snapped his fingers again, this time for his tea.

"Envy-Anger-Covetousness," he stuttered, for he never could tell the one from the other (them being women and so forth, a boy would have been different), "go and get me my tea will you!"

At this the youngest daughter rushed to be the first to do his bidding, but in her desperation she raced so impulsively that the cup rocked sideways in its saucer and the tea slopped everywhere.

"Envy-Anger-Covetousness-Pride-Gluttony," roared the Devil, but his fiery eye was on his youngest daughter, no doubt about it, and the girl trembled in her bright red dress, wondering if this was the moment she had waited for, and if now, at long last, her father would remember her name.

Glaring furiously at her the Devil tried again. "Envy-Anger-Pride," he began, and this time got as far as Lechery before his memory failed him, and with ash and frustration spouting from his nostrils he exploded: "I'm surrounded by bloody women and I canny even get my tea on time!"

At this the other daughters flurried to refill his teacup and serve up his sandwiches, but this time the youngest, seeing that she had been saved by forgetfulness, thought it better to hang back a bit.

Unfortunately for her, however, the Devil did not fail to notice that there was one among his daughters who hardly stirred an inch. And his memory creaked, and his memory strained, and his memory was suddenly restored to him.

"Sloth by name and Sloth by nature!" he roared in triumph. And Sloth hid her bright red dress behind Gluttony's bulk, and stuck her thumb in her mouth, and decided she would far rather not be special at all.

The Belly of the Whale

A grizzled cat falters on to Mona's knee and lowers itself into her lap. "Meet Sheba," she says. "She's a right guzzle-gut. None too bright, either."

Her hand sinks contentedly into the cat's fur, and Dee sinks with it, hypnotized, thinking that it really would be nice to be a child who simply is adored, who simply is, who doesn't have to try all the time and who doesn't have to fight her secret yearnings to stop, to give up, to stop running from retribution. To fall like Jonah thankfully into the warm belly of the whale.

Outside the sun is setting. Halley's Comet hangs invisible in the bright dust of Scorpio's tail. On Bondi Beach the night's vigils will be beginning: boys and girls with beers, bonfires, binoculars. She feels her narrow body lazing, rounding, spreading. Not old, so much, but tired, yes, she really is quite tired.

Whalebones. Whalebones like those which slotted into grand-mother's corsets or the strapless frocks that she and Mona used to dress up in. There was a yellow net dress, some cousin's cast-off, which only Mona had the breasts for. She used to think of slipping the bones from their sheaths, stealthily, so that the dress simply collapsed: a thrilling sort of sabotage, just the sort of trick to play on a big sister. She never did, or course, but she was tempted.

Imagine the whale's belly as an arch, boned. Imagine Jonah, then, slipping the stiff whalebones out and smothering in soft tented folds, kissing his identity goodbye.

She rubs the crease between her eyebrows again, rubs and rubs, trying to nip the image of lassitude from her mind's eye. Time and tide wait for no woman, after all. Not if she wants to be a winner. Not if she wants Mona to be a winner too. Oh, hard on herself, maybe. But what's the alternative? Lethargy?

"We could phone round," she says, rousing herself. "You know — find out about some courses for you."

Mona sets the cat aside and rises slowly, brushing hairs from her housecoat. "I've got lamb chops, do you like lamb chops?" Her face has a stubborn set which Dee doesn't remember. "Thing about me," she adds. "I've got to take things at my own pace."

Oh *well,* Dee thinks impatiently. Well then.

The lamb chops come ten minutes later, to be eaten on their laps in the living room. Dee looks at the mashed potatoes with a sinking heart. "Do you like cooking?" she asks. Dee, the picky one, propelling bright green peas round her plate.

Mona shrugs. "I've never gone great guns on cooking, I eat at work mostly."

Dee offers to help. She'll cook every day, she'll cook French, Italian, Australian if there is such a thing. Just to set an example. She imagines showing Mona how to mince chicken finely, and snip parsley; they could discuss vintages and vegetables, take long walks in the Tassie sun, and Mona's weight would soon fine down, and her pale cheeks glow brighter than rosehips.

Mona balances her plate on her knee, her fork poised. "Food Research try some pretty weird things out on us. They serve them up with garlic and what have you." She laughs. "We've had krill this week. Sort of shrimp things whales feed on. Guess they reckon on poisoning the typists first, save the eggheads for later!"

Shopping

"Don't you like fresh juice better?" Dee hints, watching Mona stock the supermarket trolley with cartons of orange squash.

Mona wrinkles her nose. "Too sour for me." Up and down the aisles they go, past packet noodles and walnut gateau mix and fat orange madeira cakes.

At the vegetable counter Dee holds up radishes, spring onions, avocados: advertisements for health.

"Just get what you fancy," Mona says discouragingly.

"But all that sugar," Dee protests, "it's so bad for you!"

Mona's eyes flicker away, and she shrugs. Turning the trolley round, she steers it towards the checkout. "Yay well, chocolate's my big hang-up, I guess."

So Mona doesn't even have the excuse of ignorance. So she's simply wasting her breath. Oh, she knows the lure of nursery food as well as anyone: treacle pudding and chocolate raisins and banana custard, specially, if you're depressed, but honestly, Mona, where's your self-discipline? Speechless, Dee fumes all the way to the carpark.

In the car Mona reaches for the small soda bottle and sips. Dee shuts her eyes and chews gum fiercely. Day by day, Mona is going to get bigger. Soon she will be the biggest baby, with her sweetened bottle, the bottle which goes everywhere, the bottle with the straw in the top. Just looking at Mona makes her want to wail. Mona's sucking and sucking which spirals like a whirlpool at the centre of her stillness.

Moral(e)

Lift log six times above head, returning to trestle. Repeat twice. Dee is running hard. Puffing. On the Family Exercise Track in the bush behind the house. On cinders.

Blood is thicker than water, Mother says, and *You'll always have each other*.

Every few hundred yards there are graded exercise spots. The bush is green and foreign around her.

Hang from metal rings and circle body clockwise, repeat anti-clockwise.

She is running. Panting. Maybe she's running away from her responsibilities. But if she storms in with her temporary zeal, slash slash, then who'll look after Mona when she's gone, just answer that. Running. Panting out steam and relief. She'd be bloody mad, wouldn't she? To consider it.

Leisure

"Thought I'd get a video for later," Mona offers. "You can hire them at the corner shop now."

There's already quite a collection on Mona's shelves: "Raiders of the Lost Ark", "Bladerunner", "Romancing the Stone". Dee scans the titles and frowns. "A video?"

Mona is flustered. "You know, only if you fancy. I wasn't sure if you . . ."

"No, okay, really, why not." In her honest opinion videos turn whole populations into passive half-wits, but here is Mona, only trying to please her. She imagines herself in front of the television for the entire evening, drugged, immobile, bulging with fantasy.

A Fall From Altitude

Like it or not, Pre-Menstrual Mean Time strikes in the middle of the night, and in the spare room Dee's whale-self wakes on a wave. Bloody women, Kerouac accuses, prodding at her with his forked harpoon until she rolls and dives for safety. And comes up on tides of tears, thinking piteously that at menstrual times above all others you need to feel special and special she does not feel, special she is not. From the bed she can see herself in the dressing-table mirror, stranded there, her belly round as Mona's pleasing nobody and her skin bursting. In a minute she'll outgrow all narrowness and then who will she be, who, if not narrow any longer? Just a blur, indistinguishable from her sisters, from the lazy ebb and furl and flow of all sad stories . . .

Dee heaves herself out of bed. On her way to the bathroom, in the hallway, she passes Mona's open door and peeks. Mona lies on her back, utterly still, she has never seen anyone alive so still. For a second her heart stops. A heart attack, an attack on the heart. Mona's arteries choked with sugar. Or else Mona has killed herself, taken sleeping pills or something, all that inertia crushing her.

Suspicious in her sleepiness, she moves closer to the bed. For surely Mona used to play tricks too? *Pretended to be dead once, to scare me.* Down in the dark and taking Dee with her. Pretended there was a man on the landing between them and the bathroom, a murdering man, the devil or someone. You'll just have to hold it in, Dee, won't you? Paralysing her.

   Dee can't move, terrified of going or staying. *You'll just have to hold it in.*

The pillows sigh. Staring at Mona in the thin moonlight, Dee sees the almost imperceptible breathing, and the faint underwater smile, as if deep down in sleep contented dreams are courting her.

Do or Dee

It's morning. Outside, Dee braces her back against the wall next to the balcony, and balances on the parapet of a terraced flowerbed where hydrangeas tower. In this position she can prune and sunbathe at the same time, although the sun silhouettes the hydrangea blooms, melding fresh blue heads with dead brown ones, so that she has to finger the petals from time to time to distinguish them. Holding the shears so high above her head makes her ache and sweat; her period grumbles in her, making her feel clumsy. Cobwebs whisper across her wrists, nose, mouth, but the adversity only spices her. She grits her teeth, liking a fight she can win. She slashes through years of neglect, works towards a perfectly limned garden. She is slashing through entropy, and that tendency of time to pass and blood to flow and love to leave and all things to fall mouldering into chaos.

Up and above, Mona nods in the balcony monotony. "Enjoying yourself, are you?"

Dee smiles through her sweat and slashes harder. She will be Mona's long knife, her thief. She is setting an example. Energy and ambition rise in tandem as her eye falls on the straggled rosebushes, the bramble runners under the balcony, the cypress tree whose branches dangerously occlude the entrance to the driveway. Never content with one task where two or three can be accomplished (brushing her teeth and combing her hair while having a pee, for instance), she wishes for eight hands, not two. She could even be a combine harvester.

Under the spokes of a revolving washing line, the cat licks a paw in the sunshine, fumbles it up over one ear. "Beats me how you ever sit still enough to write a book," Mona laughs.

"Done," Dee cries at last, throwing down the shears dramatically. Down in the bay the sea is lead blue, the sky parched to the horizon. She jumps down from the parapet and drops into a garden chair, face tilting up and back, greedy for the sun and, as the canvas chair skews under her, as the washing line and the spokes of the morning sun wheel over her, as the chair tips backwards, as she falls upside down and back-of-the-neck first on to the paved path, she sees Mona turn in slow motion, shocked hand flying to her throat.

"My God, you all right?" She descends the balcony steps, while Dee lies feet in the air, spinning still but not broken, no, just clumsy: "Yes, fine, how stupid can you get." Dee sits up, feels herself, rotates her head experimentally.

And Mona starts to laugh. "Wallop!" She flips her hand over. "You went . . . oh no . . . *Wallop!*" She does it again. Standing big over Dee, flipping her hand over, laughter shaking her.

Tourism

What can we see? We can see wallabies and wombats, we can see currawongs with their red-ringed rapacious eyes, we can see grey-haired kookaburras gulping lizards to the last inch of tail, luxuriously, throats tilted back, like old men eating oysters.

"There aren't any koalas left," Mona says at breakfast, "but would you like to see a Tasmanian Devil?"

Dee nods, but she's still aching for sleep, having woken in a mood so mournfully despairing that there must have been some dream of delight, surely, that the day broke into. Something wishful and wonderful.

They drive south, past bush blackened by summer fires, to a reserve surrounded by orchards. The keeper tells them that he is expecting a Japanese coach tour any second, if they wouldn't mind hanging on for it. They buy apples and cigarettes. Dee looks across the carpark, bleary, seeing a grey infuriating Sunday, a kiosk with souvenirs. A second or an hour, it's all the same to her, for if there was some saving vision in the dream her mind refuses to unlock it.

Enclosed by a waist-high wall, two dozen rat-like creatures which run around the keeper's booted feet, letting out short high shrieks. They have needle teeth, snouty rooting noses, fat rumps covered in salt and pepper hair. The insides of their mouths are very red. The Japanese aim their cameras, wince and giggle.

"I told you they were no oil paintings," Mona whispers beside her, as the keeper sets one of the Devils on the wall.

Dee nods heavily, working at her smile. It's incredible. The weekend has almost run out and here they are, still being polite to each other. She reads the illustrated notice in the enclosure, looks dully for a redeeming feature. Oh, I'm just depressed, period cramps, the usual, blah blah blah, it's really not worth talking about. Tidal and wordless. The Devils don't have a lot to recommend them either. You can't pet or coo over them, they have no beauty of bone structure, their temperament is quarrelsome, their parenting inadequate . . .

She leans over the wall to watch two infants harrying each other. There's a stir in the crowd, a faint foreign cry. Someone grasps the sleeve of her jacket and tugs timidly. The keeper lunges. "Look out, Miss!" He catches the Devil, holds it high in the air, its jaws snapping. "Little blighter reckoned on taking a bite out of you there!"

Back at the car, Dee starts to laugh. Bad bad bad, she thinks joyfully, biting into an apple, hard. The apple tastes of rain and sky and bark. She can't stop.

"What's eating you?" Mona asks.

"Don't you identify with those Devils, though?" Laughing still. But this time there's no running from it. A pain so fat and great coming home to her that consciousness tries to twist away. "Oh, you know." Struggling. "Awful. *Ugly.*"

"Should I?" Mona looks at her, mild, blank, quizzical. Her hand rests on the neck of the small squash bottle. She gives her distancing smile. "Being a bit hard on yourself, aren't you?"

Dee chews angrily, her skin stretched to bursting point.

"OH FOR GOD'S SAKE STOP SUCKING THAT THING MONA."

Brown apple leaves blow across the carpark, and this time there's nothing holding her together. On the deck of a ship Mona waves a blue headscarf, leaving and leaving, and all the things they weren't allowed to do or be are devils to drive her away.

Mona reaches for a cigarette, fits it into her holder. Lights it. A tear sits astonished on her cheekbone. Only her hands are shaking.

Dee is desperate.

Fight me, Mona. With your little finger.

"Yay well," Mona whispers, "I guess I need to get to grips with . . ."

Dee clutches her shoulder, her thick skin, a transgression. Faintly in the distance the Devils are still shrieking.

"Tell me about Gary, Mona."

SISTER WHALE

Once upon a time there was a whale and a boy-girl riding her. They sought treasure in a rusted chest at the bottom of the blue Pacific, treasure so deep and locked that the girl, unaided, could not dive down far enough, or stay down long enough, to open it. And so they went down, the two of them, into the salt healing sea, the boy-girl clinging to the whale's broad back, down and down, with the whale's deep belly-breath taking her. Until they came at last among the corals to the nub of the chest, and the great whale smashed the lock with one slap of her flukes. And when the lid fell back, the boy-girl saw that inside the chest was a starry starry night and a mirror cheap as tinsel but every bit as beautiful

"Ready?" Dee cries, restless at the window with the sun so high and hot out there and everything still to be achieved.

"Ready," Mona replies, scooping up her cigarette case.

> *You will take your sister down to the sea and with hooked fingers scoop a channel for the tide to flow around her brown and silver until she floats: bright and bonny of eye, slaty-blue and glistening, once in the water stately and at ease. Slithering under with relief, she noses with dolphins, but if you follow her, water not being your element will bob you to the top, thrusting you back towards air and sky, there is no other space to speak from and try as you may you will not be able to*

> *I hold her white hand, my accomplice, while with a flick of her luxuriant tail she takes me down, my big sister Britannia in a brown flowered housecoat, down into moony blue and boundless she too big for me to eat and boundless I too thin to threaten*

On the beach Mona sits serenely, smoking, with her legs straight out, while Dee runs clowning on white sand so fine it squeaks like clean hair under her bare feet, drags a sheet of seaweed from the surf, bile-green and blistered like perished rubber, and when the wind wraps it wet and toga-like around her Mona laughs. It is so marvellous when she laughs.

LUST

KATHY ACKER

LUST

"A Sailor's Slight Identity"

LUST

A SAILOR'S SLIGHT IDENTITY

Because he's alone, a sailor's always telling himself who he is:

Due to the increasing conservatism of this government, the cops're enforcing more and tighter restrictions on every area of the private sector. Even the hippies and punks're no longer rioting. Capture by the German cops means torture or, at best, slavery. Thus, in Berlin, I was an insect. I am going to describe the life of vermin.

Burroughs said that writers are insects. Without lives. Like sailors. A writer's one type of sailor, a person without human relationships.

Cold winds sweep over our dead rats; a dead terrorist's heart sits on dogshit. Mutilated police calls, advertising leaflets spell SOS. I liked watching and reading about two men stroking each other's penises. When I reached Berlin, one morning when the street beyond my window was almost the color of diarrhoeic dog turd from the rain, I saw two men who were obviously a couple. One told the other, a small bastardy-looking shit, "I'll get the groceries."

I didn't leave: I had nothing better to do than wait for someone whom I didn't know to return. About two hours later, he returned with a small bag. I wanted to follow him back to his room; I didn't; I knew that following him would be useless.

Through condoms and orange peels, mosaics of newspapers floating in small pools of water and piss, down into the ooze with gangsters in concrete and pistols pounded flat to avoid ballistic detection.

I like looking at men who've got muscles. Short bodies. These men look like bastards. They're the ones who act, who can act.

They give their energy. When I look at one, I have him and I lean my head right back into his chest. Between his large hand and his stomach, there, it's warm. There I'm safe. Since he makes me safe, I'll do anything for him. I know this sexuality, who I am, is nothing to be proud of: I am almost nothing. But I can't hate myself.

The muscular man's erection was hardening. The two men kept their mouths soldered together with tongues either crushed or sharp tips in contact. A knife cannot cut through another knife. Neither dared to place his tongue on the other's cheek, for a kiss is a sign of vulnerability. By mistake a pair of eyes now and then caught the other pair of eyes. Then they hid. Snakes. Tongues were as hard as metal. The pricks are harder than tongues.

If I'm to go on living, I have to accept my sexuality.

I never knew my dad. He had left my mother for good six months before I was born. He had never wanted to meet me.

Though very little of my time is devoted to fucking, often none for months, I think constantly about sex and sexuality. It was about 4:20 A.M. in a Communist Chinese hotel in Germany. Two narrow and separated beds were nailed to the floor. There was a thin grey carpet. There were two small towels. There was a wardrobe. There was a table. There were four upright chairs. There was a telephone. I had left my ship about two days ago.

A man, whom I knew slightly, a criminal type, phoned. He told me that I was lonely and he'd be good for me. I wanted to ask him questions which I was to shy to ask a stranger—

(1) Do you want to fuck me in the ass?

(2) Do you want to fuck me in the ass more than once?

Three weeks later I met this man in another town in Germany. His body was short. His muscles slightly inclined to fat. After two hours we kissed. I continued to kiss him harder faster, with rising and more cunningly, here there, quick little pecks as my tough, very wide lips moved nearer his left ear. Every animal finds a home or dies. Finally I placed my tongue in an ear which was dirty.

The tongue moved around the thick ear. I placed my cheek against his teeth because I wanted him to bite me hard. Like big warm animals hug, he held me in arms as wide as my torso.

He was a sailor.

I tried to grab his huge head and pull it down as if I were wrestling. At the same time the rest of me was pressing into him, especially his lower body, and twining my legs around his so that our genitals could meet and rub through the wool.

In this warmth which we had created we remained together. I kept kissing and rubbing the bullet head, then kissing his male skin everywhere. Rubbing the skin or mind into need.

Want rose up, the sailor.

At last I found myself about to ejaculate. I wanted to prolong this need, whose appearance was physical, into total desperation, into the most desperate need which is possible, that is, not possible. But it was impossible to remain living in the impossible.

No longer could I distinguish between lust and love. I wanted to smear KY over his, Mick's, cock. Rusty barges, red brick buildings, graffiti of dead anarchists on the wall, only because he was going to hurt me, I fantasized the possibility that he would hurt me. Why do I get off on being rejected? I don't care. Cut off a leg and another limb grows stronger. Our generation came out of mutilation. We wear our mutilations as badges; wearing badges is the only possibility we have for human love. I fantasized that his penis was not very long and was thick. A penis that looked like a boxer, if a boxer could look like a penis.

When I had first noticed him in Hamburg, I had been sitting next to him. I remember that I looked down and saw a large lump in old grey pants. The thighs were heavy and spread apart, as if the hill would rise up in between ... At the same time as I saw this, I noticed I was staring at the lump. I wouldn't have been conscious of my fascination if I had thought that there were any sexual attraction between us.

At last I found myself about to ejaculate. I let the hand that was perching on Mick's shoulder slide down his back till it reached the buttocks. The buttocks were moving. I put my hand around this quivering, still clothed flesh and took possession of it. I slipped my hand up, and under the trouser belt and the white undershirt in front. I touched the penis. I forced myself to do what I wanted to do.

I was in that being or state where only sex matters.

My other hand took hold of one of his thick hands and forced it to touch my penis. Dolphins leapt about the prow and flying fish scattered before us almost in golden showers. Mick stroked the naked penis under the wool trousers, then on his own accord unbuttoned my flap. Dead leaves falling, jagged slashes of blue sky where the boards curled as if from fire apart. Mick squeezed my penis so hard that I whispered for a suck. Mick bent down only the upper part of his body and parted his lips. Violet twilight yellow-gray around the edges, color of human brains. While he was kneeling in front of me, Mick was sucking my cock so red it was obscene.

Whereas the slums in Hamburg are the slums of its sailors, Berlin is a big slum. For everyone. Except the tourist section which is fake shit for the foreigners. Just as the USA is fake shit because of a few people's manipulations. But playgrounds die. The English Labour Party holds hands and sings "Auld Lang Syne".

The Barrio Chino, a section in Berlin only known to Berlin's dedicated alcoholics and speed shooters, is a geographical foulness inhabited, not by Spanish sailors nor by the American Merchant Marine, nor by Turks, but by those who have been separate so long from their birthplaces or anything resembling home, they are nationless. As long as they're alive, lost. The Barrio Chino is a place for drifters. Loneliness rather than sex has become the last vestige of capitalism. Loneliness is both a disease and a cause of personal strength and pride.

These sadistic and masochistic drifters resemble the criminals who lived in the American and German urban conglomerates prior to the emergence of crime as international monopoly.

Before human relationships degenerated into piss. Before the filth and disorder of the Barrio Chino. Long ropes hang between sailors' legs.

Sardine can cut open with scissors . . . shoehorn has been used as spoon . . . dirty sock in a plate of moldy beans . . . toothpaste smear on washstand glass . . . cigarette butt ground out in cold scrambled eggs . . . the children of the Barrio Chino.

An apartment at no. 10–11 Bayernallee on Holy Sunday, November 10, 1974, when all the virgins were singing loneliness. Someone rang its doorbell. Through the intercom, the doorbell ringer said he was delivering flowers. (The owner of this flat, Günter von Drenkmann, President of the Superior Court of Justice and Berlin's senior judge, was celebrating his 64th birthday.) When the door was opened, one of the youths outside pushed the door wide open. Another kid shot at Drenkmann three times and hit him twice.

Then all of these kids escaped in one Peugeot and one Mercedes. They obviously had stolen the cars. The old judge died.

The first penis I saw in Berlin was so beautiful I died. Before that I had thought that I was living in boredom. With this I found a community. Penises were lice. Sometimes they were crabs through whom I could see. Water seeped through the rotting walls upward into more rotting materials. The flesh melted into ooze. I wanted to tear down these walls, the ooze, to enter fully into Mick. To mingle in the way that no flesh can mingle. Mick was my mirror, my wall. I knew for a moment I was his. But the owners of the walls, the landlords, wouldn't let us tear them down. Owners hate sailors. Even owners who believe in liberalism, for democracy's other side is crime.

Every now and then, for instance when the President of the United States came to town, the Barrio Chino held a riot. Hatred made us erect.

Mick and I lived together for six months. He wasn't my greatest fuck, but I didn't care because he was the scum I wanted. I had no family and he wasn't going to be one, but for six months I got fucked. We parted for good without a reason.

Two nights after we had parted, in a bar whose walls and ceiling were aluminum, I picked up another sailor. As the sailor was sliding a hand up to my testicles from the back, I strangled him in the bar's back room. No one in the bar cared about my strangulation. Islands isolated in madness. I watched his life ebbing (refuse) under the pressure of my clenched, tightened fingers (refusés), watched the sailor die with mouth agape (refused) tongue out (speechless), watched the crisis of my solitary pleasures (refusal). City of flesh shrivelled in aluminum bars, yellow couches, tables covered in speed dust. I killed him because I needed to be rejected by you who are alive. Only then would I find a community of those who are like me.

By murdering I raise myself out of the death in which I'm living. When I murdered the sailor, a miraculous wave broke into the silence of my ears (no one to whom to talk), the silence of my mouth (no one to whom to talk): the world started humming.

At this point I had no friends. The only thing there is to talk about now is isolation. Though my murdering had come from isolation — isolation is always insupportable — my murdering also announced my isolation to the world and so provided the first step toward destroying isolation. Afterwards I could only turn to other murderers. To those who realized they were sick. We are the failures on, not the governors of, this earth. Consciousness of our failure allowed us to be friends. The diseased fear only poverty. For all else is theirs and not to be feared: isolation, the ravages of sexual needs, ravaging sexual need, misunderstanding, autism, visual and audial hallucination, paranoia.

This night which has lasted for a long time I want to say that I cannot stand isolation anymore. The only way I see out of isolation is murder. Which makes isolation. This, in a sense, is my ode to the Baader-Meinhof, a group of kids who didn't fully consider the consequences of going against the law of the land, of ownership, became mad. This endless night.

Here I am alone.

In Berlin, something beside isolation happened. In the middle of a night. I drove around in a car with two other people with a cassette blaring out Marc Almond and Neubauten. In that country where the bourgeoisie are so stolid, they are immovable fairytales: isolated from the world and from myself, doubly isolated, I found friends.

The next day the cops tried to find the sailor's, Joachim's, murderer. I didn't feel guilty because I had murdered a Jew. The cops decided that a black man, another sailor, whose name was the name of a pariah, had murdered my sailor.

Perhaps it was out of guilt that the court sentenced Jonah to an early execution. Jonah was executed.

Now, I wanted to forget. Not my murder, but the world that had wrongly condemned Jonah, the world that condemned my murder, the world that, or rather who, caused isolation. I wanted to disappear. I wanted to disappear from this world into the night. I knew that it was impossible to kill myself.

Weil er mein Freund ist, liebt er mich. The cops weren't going to learn that I had actually murdered the sailor because the cops were snouts. The next man I fucked was a cop. I insisted that what I wanted most was that he pierce my throat as far as possible and fill it with slime.

I won't kiss but I get off on sucking the prick of a man whom I detest. Because I'm penetrating myself. When I was sucking the dick's prick, I was able to go beyond myself. At the same time, I was frightened: I would lose control and bite the cock too hard, which wouldn't be a bad thing, but, on the other hand, cops are human. Sucking this hot cock made my own despair and nothingness or my death apparent to me.

How black Berlin.

While I was thinking this in the act of sucking him off, the cop moaned, "I'm a cop. I'm a cop and I'm a creep. Cause I make it with guys. *Weil er mein Freund ist, liebt er mich.* I'm homosexual. I make it with every punk I can get. Then I shove the kid into jail so that I can have him whenever I want. I put the kid in jail cause that's what I like. I like putting the kid into jail after making him do what both of us want. My hands control his mouth."

The more this cop confessed through his mutterings, confessed to a sailor he didn't know, and it didn't matter in the slime of Berlin, what slime he was, the more he became a hero to me. After only a little while more I would do anything for this big man. I loved being like this. It was like being someone else. Or being someone. In an unkown place of wonder. I would grovel at the cop's feet and, then, like a puppy, try to nip the cop's ankles. Big cops wear boots because they ride BMWs. When his sperm was visible and dead, the cop and I had nothing to say to each other.

Nothing new was happening in the city. It was time to leave. It's not that the Nazis had ruined a world. The Nazis had changed nothing. Dead cops don't fuck; death breeds only death. My nostrils were stinking of the smegma in my belly and the smegma on the streets so it was time to leave.

I went back to my ship where I carried out my duties impeccably. For theres no reason not to do exactly what I'm told to do even by scum.

Back in Berlin the cop rose in his work. He became a lieutenant. Seeing that his career was beginning, finally sure of himself to be master of his domain, decay: he began to do as he pleased.

Bits of what I wrote at sea:

> I find myself alone. I'm safe because the ocean surrounds me like when I was a child. I no longer have to be an animal crazy in its foraging for food. Society appears to be largely composed of extremists and habitual criminals not normal human animals subjects or citizens of respectable states. But

I have no more community here cause sailors aren't usually
murderers: sailors are nothing. I have had to decide,
because I'm on the edge of suicide, that loneliness, like
poverty, is a test. I no longer understand anything that is
happening to me.

I wrote this about my murder:

When that grief that is beyond tears, that tears the griever
apart, that grief over a human death, fades: emptiness
remains. The shock that a demi-god, one to whom one has
given suck, can die becomes only the shock of death: the
dead person *cannot* be dead. Death, above all, is impossible.
That is: unthinkable.

Besides shock, all the other to-do surrounding murder or
political assassination is a hypocritical way of pretending
that the demi-god or human cannot be replaced in our
society *which is actually a world of interchangeable puppets.*
Of pretending that there are still human individuals, that
these individuals still make history, when in fact all that we
individuals — sailors — can now do is is wish to act, exert
ineffective wills, talk endlessly about human morality (do
animals have morality?), when in fact the autonomous
mechanisms of social repression have been and are being
reproduced in every individual.

A world of interchangeable puppets . . . unless you starve
. . . the autonomous mechanisms of social repression . . .
unless you starve . . . inevitably reproduced in every
individual . . .

. . . an eroticized state . . .

In this society of total, not so much conformity, but
homogenization, pasteurization beyond what the fifties'
sociologists envisaged, we're making signs to each other
that we're unlike by displaying disease or murdering. It's
hard to be friends. Though we both know we're evil, I

wonder whether or not we'll be friends. I make mistakes, often out of impatience, by imagining that there's camaraderie when there's not.

I wrote this about romanticism which comes after murder:

> I first came to Berlin when I was twenty. I found whatever I was looking for there, though I still couldn't name it. I first came to Berlin when I was twenty for some reason which I didn't know. Before I was in Berlin, I stole motorcycles and bashed them up in Munich. They didn't like me there because I'm very quiet. Too quiet. Until they show they hate me and then my back's against the wall and then I go mad. I become violent. I hate most of all being shut up or bored. Say that I hate everyone and every social thing. Me: I believe in romanticism. Romanticism *is* the world. Why? Because there's got to be something. There has to be something for we who are and know that we're homeless.

When I returned, not to Berlin, but to Hamburg in the midst of the fog of the beginning of winter, to the road that runs right above its river and docks, a castle which never existed and a fountain which is really a sewer, a gust of wind far sweeter and more fragrant than any red rose carried the smell of shit and floating soil like a tongue into my nostril.

It was late at night. As yet there were no dreams. I wondered when dreams would come to me, when the real dreams would come, dreams of something besides sailors. I wondered where they were. Like a man who wants to sleep and can't, so tries without success to know sleep. Wondered when the muscles of my face would be released, when my eyelids would blink more slowly, when the last light would die. When soft, gentle, and not just from weariness, you would lay on your back. Still in your sailor's uniform.

Tender and gentle, you then run your hands between my buttocks as if you're loving me there. Out of modesty, a form of fear perhaps, frightened that your prick is soiled by my asshole shit, I clean it with my free hand. My other hand, already seeking your hair in order to touch it, meets the face and strokes the cheek instead.

No love can be expressed between us. Love doesn't exist between us. We know only our varied musculature which has developed out of pain. You say that only fiction or language could inform us that we love each other. Perhaps this is true. But it's for other reasons that we understand what we mean when we speak together, our grunts, our solipsisms. Without the musculature which comes from pain no one is understood. With both hands clinging, one to an ear, the other to your hair, I wrench your head away from my axis which is getting harder.

Whenever you have sex with someone, you partially become each other.

After this sailor had finished cocksucking, I strangled him. Abandoned by parents, by friends, by America, by the pricks I had sucked, I knew that above all I hated, not death, but giving up to death.

DEAD PEOPLE DON'T FUCK

El marinero degollado
Cantaba el oso de agua que lo había de estrechar.

There were three poets. The three poets were ugly old men. They had once been hippies, but they were no longer hippies. They thought that without their visions, this city would dissolve. Without their dreams, the city would dissolve. This city is dissolving anyway. Being into love, the poets had nothing to celebrate.

They were just like snakes who, not having anything to eat, eat their own tails. When snakes eat themselves out, they think they are the only thing there is. More and more of the people are hungry.

There was a falling-down church. The church was a hideout for Puerto Rican terrorists. A young woman leapt up from one of the church pews, there weren't many of them, as if her ass was full of tracks, but it was just tacky. She was lean and brown; her gown was pink; she began to slink just like a slinky fat rat forwards and back:

I'm gwine down to de river
Set me down on de ground
If the blues overtake me,
Gon' jump overboard and drown.

It was one of the weekly readings in the Puerto Rican terrorist church.

Not this.

The church was called "St. Marks-in-the-Bowery". In an urban environment, a "bowery" is a bum refuge. Bums of all kinds including sexual genders lived on its doorsteps and everywhere inside and outside this church. The Puerto Ricans lived underneath the graves. Every now and then a gang of children dug up a grave. Since the bums lived everywhere in the city, they were taking over the city just like the cockroaches had already taken the walls.

One of the three old men was just about to begin to read his poetry. In his mind, or in the depths of his soul, what he was about to begin to read was jazz. Because he liked garbage, he wrote poetry by picking phrases out of the cultural garbage cans — newspapers, sex mags, tv coverage, great poems, everything else — and stringing these phrasings together according to inaudible musical rhythms. He would have been reading to a sax, but the saxophonist had died ten years before. The poet didn't notice much outside him and he didn't have opinions.

Not this.

The church's audience were friends (other old poets), students, and bums. The students weren't yuppies, but revolutionary radicals and non-revolutionary radicals who aspired to the radicalness of bums. A few of the latter radicals had come in order to burn the church down. The bums had come in to escape the cold. The church wasn't heated. No one gave a damn about the reading.

Just as the old poet was about to read, a bum said, "Ah. Ah feels like cutting me some white motherraper's throat." For a moment, someone was silent.

"We'll burn down the church," one student whispered to another.

Not this.

"Kill all the poets cause they're dead," another student who wasn't a poet said in a slightly louder voice.

"I'll say! Cause religion sucks!"

"No, it doesn't cause poets should be crucified."

Dick, the old poet who was about to read, ignored these catcalls, knowing he was above them, being a poet, mainly cause he was frightened. So he stammered out, "Pope . . . Pope Pius the Sixth . . . Pope Pope." Maybe he thought that he was more famous than he was.

Not this.

Then remembering, then becoming lost in the wonder of his imagination, he started reading:

> give us all honest work
> to fuck every girl here
> Annie Joanne Suzie Bern
> I suppose
> the main thrust is
> knowledge
> Cordelia sucked off Lear
> daddy came too late

death, you come
no system
above meaningless tragedy
any other organ

Just as a revolutionary student pulled out a Magnum in order to halt the advance of immoral apolitical destructive artistic nonsense, one of the other old men, since he didn't notice the gun, limped toward the podium in order to extricate his friend from the masses' growing hostility. Tall and thin, this poet, pasty-faced, three hairs away from bald, for years his mouth frozen by speed into a smile, signalled to his friend to shut up.

At the same time, a bum walked into the church.

Not this.

There were many bums in the church. That's how society is. This bum appeared visible because his right hand was holding his left hand and his left hand wasn't holding anything like an arm. He wasn't a writer. His left foot stood opposite to the way it should have stood. He walked, as much as he was able, to the backmost pew and perched up there like a great huge vulture.

Now Dick began to read a love poem to his wife:

There is no way
to find me
while I find many
cunts, my Muse . . .

The bum took out his tiny cock and began to rub its head as if it was a dog. Finally, the students noticed that something was happening.

The bum, paying attention to the attention he and his dog were drawing, cried out to Dick, "Give to the poor."

Dick was now invoking Venus for some reason or other, probably a poetic one.

Not this.

"Shit and fuck," one of the non-revolutionary students said to another, "that's the bum who thinks he's a cop. He's always trying to arrest another bum. Here ya' go," the student threw a dead animal heart into the cop's lap.

"Come to me, my lady," said Dick.

"Give to the poor," murmured the cop as the dead heart hit his other cheek.

At this signal for war, over a hundred bums, who had forgotten to pay attention to the first signal, swarmed into the church in order to further their plan of taking over the city. Churches are major property owners. Thinking that all these new people were here to hear his poetry, Dick exclaimed:

> you took my love so tenderly
> with lips.

The bum in the back proceeded to show how.

Not this.

Mayor Koch, various church officials, and other government and real-estate agents were walking through this church in order to get rid of poverty and clean up the filth who were left. One of the real-estate men, casually dressed in bluejeans, said, "Poetry is shit."

The crowd agreed with him.

"Shit," yelled the members of the religious congregation.

"Shit."

"Shit."

Not this.

"Let's elect our own mayor," a bum said. Poverty changes the mind.

Cut to the quick and deeply hurt, Mayor Koch and his cohorts, criminal and otherwise, scrambled through walls of bums and ran away from the church's graves.

Now came the election of their Mayor of New York. In order to maintain democratic procedure, the students smashed one of the stained glass panels over the altar. The bums watched other people work. Whoever desired to be mayor would stick his or her face through the broken glass. The populace could choose the image they wanted to rule them.

Not this.

The poor want their own mirror. The world was created in the image of God.

Dick was reading his poetry.

"I'm just trying to sell coca-cola," one of the bums explained. "I'm not doing anything illegal." This bum was a big bum who once had had some muscle. Now his clothes didn't do much to hide his lack of muscles. "I dropped into this church just so I's could patronize my customers."

"You're under arrest." The bum who thought he was a cop.

"No, I ain't, cause I ain't done nothin' wrong."

Not this.

"He doesn't want to arrest you," another bum explained to the coca-cola dealer. "He just wants some coke to put between his girlfriend's legs."

The bum who thought he was a pig flicked open a switch and slashed the upper half of the coke dealer's arm.

The poets except for Dick left the church because they didn't want to vote.

Not this.

"Coke's an evil drink," one explained. "It destroys the human mind."

The first candidate for mayoralty was sticking his head through the broken glass. He was a man. The upper half of the face looked like a fox's immediately after a wolf's eaten it. The whites of his eyes were red. The lower half was all mouth. Lips composed of red mucus membrane covered by white pustules stretched over the whole.

Not this.

Even though this one looked like a poet, the mass didn't want him. He didn't look like he had cancer.

There was some blood on the floor.

The next contestant was old enough to be a politician, so he had no sexual gender much less sex and, besides that, he, or it was dead. Just as if it had cancer. Cancer-Nose. Some uneducated bum yelled things at this face in the hope that it would die.

Not this.

"Coffin-fucker!"

"Infidel!"

Many Muslims live in New York City.

The next image was that of an English rose. The image of an English rose is more beautiful, fragile, than that of a poet, but the poet's is more metaphysical. John Donne, the poet, wrote:

> Since so, my minde
> Shall not desire what no man else can finde,
>   I'll no more dote and runne
> To pursue things which had indammag'd me.

Moreover, this face was deader than the dead man's face, for this face contained a dead soul. Hippies fuck a lot. The populace wasn't bothered to vote anymore.

"She doesn't have any tits!"

Not this.

Dick, the only poet left, was so upset by the anti-feminism that he had decided to show that poetry is more powerful than politics.

> cunt ass-fucking cuntface cunthead cunt-hair smidgen tad cunt-lapper muff-diver cunt-lapping cunt meat cunt-struck diddle finger-fuck quiff roundheel quim pussy pussy-whipped asstail eatin' stuff wood pussy pussy butterfly pussy posse twat box clit clit-licker button puta dick clipped dick does a wooden horse have a hickory dick donkey dick limp-dick step on it dick-brained dick head dickey-licker screw goat fuck put the screws to someone throw a fuck into

someone rag curse chew the fat on the rag take the rag off the bush randy rim ream cocksucker twink skosh smegma suck suck ass cocksucker suck face suck off blow scum scumbag rubber scumsucker scupper sucker suck-and-swallow piss eyes like pissholes in the snow full of piss and vinegar not to have a pot to piss in panther piss a piss hard-on piss-hole bandit piss bones piss pins and needles piss-proud pisser tickle the shit out of someone shit crap poo does a bear shit in the woods doodle-shit eat shit full of shit have shit for brains holy shit horse shit shit-hole shit-hunter shit-locker shittle-cum-shaw like pigs in clover like shit through a tin horn like ten pounds of shit in a five pound bag piece of shit pile of shit scare the shit out of someone skin rubber condom get under someone's skin press the flesh

Though he hated feelings and cunts, he continued this poem:

O muse! Female muse!
Our children no longer see
no longer care
for dreams.
Syphilis lies on their face;
herpes on our testicles.
My heart has closed up
scared to exist.

Doe- or black-eyed pre-pubescent whores stood on the street-corner outside this church, swapped obscenities with the twitching junkies. The methadone center was four blocks away. Gangs of slightly older muggers crouched in the narrow alleyways between the church and the slim buildings, not yet architecturally gentrified, but soaring up in rent every month. Pigeons died. The teenagers were waiting to rob someone, but there was no one to rob except each other and that wasn't much fun. In the gutters, young kids played "Junkie" and "Whore". Uncollected torn garbage cans, rotting vegetables, broken glass, used condoms, crushed beer and coke cans, dog and human piss and shit against the bottoms of the buildings. Big-tit moms, images of the Holy Virgin Mary, standing at the edges of the tenements, talked about God, unemployed, men, hunger, disease, religion, and Jews.

Not this.

"I ain't God," a man said as he showed his face through the broken glass inside the church.

"He ain't got no tits!"

Orange hair would have sprouted out of this man's mongoloid head if he had any hair. Instead, he had a few brains. A sole strand of gray spittle fell below his chin. Just like Ronald Reagan's hair if Ronald Reagan had any real hair. Or Nancy's if she had real hair on her cunt. His face was actually ugly because it was the color of a dead person's who's been hibernating in the East River for ten days. They say that alligators crawl out of the sewers into that river and have to have their stomachs pumped. The East River's sister is the Thames and the dead are dead. Dead people don't fuck. Just like my mom when she was alive. Vomit would have been prettier than the collection of characteristics on this face. Only prettiness is no criterion for high literary quality. His was the face of a literary patriarch, for his wrinkles resembled a compilation of Mr Reagan's, Margaret Thatcher's, and the asshole of a purple-assed baboon who's just been diarrhoeic. Man descended from the monkey.

Not this.

The populace of bums and students liked this one so they clapped for a long time and hard for him. In this manner, they elected their own Mayor. As soon as they had voted him in, they forgot about him which shows bums are dumb.

The living gargoyle didn't reply to any of this because he couldn't reply because he didn't have a tongue.

"Steal away to Jesus," one bum replied for him, "steal away to

Jesus," as his meaty black bones stole a wallet away and then skipped the light fantastic on one of his other bones.

Not this.

Since there was a certain lack of money among all but the rich in New York City, some of the bums were female. One of the females, while she was crying, looked at a bum and said, "I've got to say how much I want someone to care for me and I thought it was you. But it wasn't. It isn't." Crying.

"Because what I want is not what you want."

She raised her bald head up. "If a person's ugly, not evil or malicious, just ugly, everyone rejects that person. Countries ban that person. West Germany, a country in which men drink piss at parties, bans that person. That person now cannot stop being ugly and so is unrelievedly ugly.

"No one's ugly to themselves. Cause you don't see yourself. As far as seeing yourself goes: you're only seen. So an ugly person is ugly everywhere at all times. That's what ugliness's about."

Not this.

It seemed to the Mayor of New York that he was so ugly, he could not speak. So he looked for a shiv.

When a white student saw the black man looking for a shiv, he shot the ugly man. The ugly man's face contorted as he flopped on it into the lap of a bag-lady. His ugly face fell on her hand and bit it.

"Lesbian!" the bag-lady yelled, jumped up, and stamped on her mayor. "Perverts ought to be shot."

Not this.

Two more bums leaned down and turned the just-living gargoyle over on to his back; one tied one of his old Eton ties around the bleeding hand. The other stuck one of the pew legs in to tighten the tourniquet. The bum's other arm had been shot off.

The bum who had inserted the pew leg carefully into the hole looked up and found the bag-lady's pussy. "You're a bum."

"No, she's not," the other bum told him. "She's a he."

Not this.

At this revelation of the transvestism lying rank in their ranks, the coca-cola dealer stood up, though his body was tottering, and proclaimed, "Jes' sit down, folks. All of you sit down. The coke'll be here sooner than a dead man can hear a pin drop. So everyone go back to his seat and pay up. We've called the fuzz so the coke'll be protected."

Not this.

And the sailor moved out to sea.

TOO NAKED

Dead time. A few not only leafless, but almost branchless trees stand in front of water which might be stone. Three large swans step out of the stone, shake themselves off, raise themselves up, living malignant monsters, as beautiful as the dying trees. They're looking for food which doesn't exist. The soil in front of them has been shoved and grooved into lumps by the feet of humans who no longer exist.

The sailor, Xovirax, speaks:

the judgement of Paris

I didn't wait for work to come. I got the first plane out of New York. On board I sat next to a boxer. He was slight for a boxer and had blond hair. He came back with me for a drink to the flat in London which another sailor had lent me. I thought how glad I was to be out of New York. He took off my clothes and didn't take his off. He told me to speak to him without asking him questions and he didn't reply in any way to anything that I said. I was unable to speak in such circumstances though I don't understand why. Then he told me to jerk myself off while he watched me and didn't watch me, without caring. He put an ungreased hand into my asshole and lifted me above his head. Every one-night-stand or man in a one-night-stand is like every other one-night-stand or man in a one-night-stand because the sex in a one-night-stand is without time and only time allows value.

For years I've been denying my own sexuality. I've been looking for what or whom I can't find.

What I want is what the boxer gave me. I didn't know how to reconcile this (something) with the fact of a one-night-stand (nothing).

I who have murdered.

"Tonight," the boxer said, "you're going to be dead. Tomorrow I'll be the one who's dead." Picking up my head, he added, "sailors who have short hair want to be hit."

after you cut off all my hair the rest of the upper part of my body you didn't touch also the lower part except to shove your fingers into my asshole I didn't know how many you got in there enough to carry me around by my asshole I guess you're a Grecian boxer though being a sailor I'm not well-educated though I've read a lot loneliness on the sea etc: you lifted me up by my asshole and carried me into a dark room. "I'm going to fetch another prisoner who's in the chicken coop in back I hope he won't put up too much of a fight he must trust me because I'm his policeman." you left me alone in the room.

I obediently lay there and waited for you to return or not to return.

a memory came to me I'm a kid I'm squiggled up against the doorway to my father's and mother's bedroom I hear them talking about me SHE says, "Xovirax's so bad, he can't change." The WIMP agreed with her I was bad.

Then I heard you saying, "Let the accused rise have you anything to say in your own behalf?"

"It doesn't matter what I say," I said to you, "cause you aren't listening. You love me and you don't care about me."

"We'll chose the tortures," lots of voices said, "but first we have to invent the crimes. He's so small he's so pitiful even disgusting this sailor. He's not just anything. You can say and do anything to him. He's so contemptible, he wouldn't react. He isn't worth having a crime."

"He isn't worth punishing."

"No!" I cried cause absence's the worst punishment of all. But since you weren't in the room to hear me, it didn't matter what I said.

The boxer came back into the room. "OK. You pinched my jackknife."

"I didn't pinch your jackknife."

"how come I found it under your pillow."

"you did not you're a liar."

the boxer pinched me, "besides that you stole my Good Humor bar and ate it."

I couldn't bear this torture so I passed out. While I was passed out, he stuck his cock up my asshole and I came.

when you're not here I can't decide whether you're not here because you don't care about me or you're not here because you like to hurt me. there're people in this world who like to hurt other people. they're the only people who can touch me.

it's either a fact or a common belief that every mother loves her child. when I was a child, I couldn't tell whether or not my mother loved me. she hated me, but because she was my mother, I couldn't believe that she hated me. ambiguity is more painful to me than hatred.

Night after night I lay alone in that room. The boxer didn't return. I decided that he didn't care about me. I decided that he was breaking me so that life could come out and be joyful. I decided that he didn't care what he was doing to me. He was killing me. "Tonight you're going to be dead."

on the third night the boxer came back to me like Jesus Christ and untied my bonds "let the accused state," he said, "his full name age occupation permanent address because the judge has blond hair he's a German or a germ," giving a tug to the elastic band of his briefs reaching inside bringing forth sticky bubblegum used condoms Mars bars half-sucked lollipops snap crackle pop

"but I can't be a criminal if I'm dead."

"if the accused speaks once more out of turn I'm going to shove his purple tongue backwards up his nostrils so he has to give me a ream job through his nostrils"

"your asshole's smellier than my nostrils." I wanted to say this to my accuser, but he was bigger than I was. instead I moaned.

"silence in this court! disrespect will cost the disrespectful! let he who's accused and accused and accused now step forward. hmph. hmph. hmph."

I couldn't step forward cause my legs were still tied up with bubblegum which was unfair *I didn't know my crime.*

"step forward and show the court the hairs in your asshole."

I waited for Tonto to rescue me.

I waited for a long time.

Then it was morning. You said, "I've decided." You took up my head and put it on your cock. It took you two minutes to dribble a few sperm drops down my gullet. "Bye bye."

some sort of trial

1 child: You can't go. Don't I get a chance to confess? Don't I get a chance to say I'm guilty? Why don't you give me a chance to acknowledge my vicious and mysterious crimes? Can't I be a traitor? Can't I be punished forever? Can't I be an iron chain? I don't know the difference between being punished with iron chains and being an iron chain cause I'm stupid. Won't you fuckin' give me a chance you're so mean.

2 child: No, you can't confess. Wanting to confess to crimes you did and crimes you didn't do doesn't make sense. I care so much about you that what you want, punishment, hurts me.

1 child: But I want to confess. For years, cause I haven't confessed, I've gotten nothing. Cause I haven't confessed,

nothing touches me. It isn't fair! Now I'm going to confess to everything . . .

2 child: Do you know what'll happen to you if you confess in court to a serious crime? Death . . . destruction . . . pain. You can't now even watch a needle go into a cat in a film.

1 child: I know. It's horrible. I'm horrible. I'm worse than horrible. I'm evil. But boredom's more boring than evil and you've proven your boringness. So now it's my turn: I'm a pirate and I'm a murderer and I'm running after a man who isn't running after me and laying my body under his feet so he can trample me up and the feminists're watching. And all trampled up by him and his friends, I'll be laying in the piss in the gutter the ocean I don't want to drown glub glub not today maybe tomorrow.

2 child: No matter what dreadful . . . unimaginable crimes you can confess to, no one's every going to love you. Do what you want; you'll never get what you want.

1 child: You gonna have to kill me by drowning me in the ocean where there are lots of living and dead sailors all of whom have big things between their legs.

2 child: OK, fatso, now I've heard your confession and you really have convinced me that you're a suppurating pussy if there is any Justice in this court, according to the good old-time American system of equality and liberalism, you're going to be buried in sand like girls always do to boys. No, first boys try to ignore the existence of girls so the girls try to kiss them. The boys run panic-stricken from female caresses the girls chase them into deeper sands and capture them. That's how girls get back at pirates. You're not really a girl, are you, fatso?

1 child: I'm not fat that's not fair you've got to torture me some other way not by always refusing to give me food I'm sick of not getting any food you're the one who loves not giving anything

2 Child: I don't even remember the subject of this trial. Oh,

yes. The subject in front of this court is a sailor who's in love
with a man he doesn't know.
1 child: Yes, that's true.

The two children in pajamas, sitting in a bunk, facing each other,
made faces at each other and tried to scare each other by
throwing the light of flashlights in each other's chins, but only
created illusions of skulls.

I saw no way of making them agree.

alternations of reality and childhood

As soon as the boxer had come slightly in my mouth, he had said
goodbye. I was left alone like an open asshole. I want a cock, a fist
up my asshole. I want reality that lies, like everything lies, on the
surface of the butcher's shop's table where the cuts of meat stink
more than they wait.

I had to transform this situation so that I could deal with it. I
had to make my imagination real. I needed the boxer to get my
sexuality. People who are absent, like imagined people or dead
people, aren't real.

I needed a weapon to fight him. To get him back. To destroy
absence. I knew absence before I was born. I decided to give
death a shove where it hurt most.

I remembered that I had lived with a woman. In the sixth year
she informed me she was leaving me I said I'd do anything and
be anything so she wouldn't leave she left me.

Give death a shove where it hurts the most.

Nothing happens unless it's real. To pit oneself by means of a
weapon, muscularity, against death is to have value. For it must
be sufficient to transfer to the world of flesh what, since I'm
scared, is more safely, more easily done in the imaginative world.

My only weapon against the boxer seemed to be my muscularity. But I had not idea what this muscularity — these muscles

which run along the shoulder bones, growing thicker as they reach certain places in the arms, the pecs which easily flex, the tightened buttocks which can allow a greaseless hand to move easily between them — what these well-developed muscles like mad children have to do with another person.

I had no way of reaching the boxer. He had given me neither an address nor a phone number. I had to wait for him to touch me. If he was going to. I find waiting unbearable because it makes me passive and negates me. I hate being nothing. He didn't care about me. A man who didn't care about me was making me nothing. I remembered I had sworn to let no one touch me. Now I decided, if I was going to destroy death, I would have to be dead. I didn't know whether or not the boxer cared about me.

Though suicide's the opposite of muscularity, it's muscularity that allows suicide.

The boxer arrived one night unexpectedly.

"actually you're not a real pussy," he whispered while lying on my belly first he fucked me behind but actually his cock couldn't get hard, "you're an asshole you know why?" maybe he was making himself hard by jerking himself off "cause you're lying on your ass your name is barley raspberry red and twisted candy lemon yellow hole" then he took my mouth and put it to his cock

his cock rigid thick as a candle funny bump in the middle it shoots dripping wax splashes into my mouth then drops out its drool all over the place the mattress on which we're lying's a mess.

as soon as he comes two drips in my mouth then splatters spatters all over the place he mutters "I'm going to go" which is no fun at all besides he's already done that so I anwer "instead of leaving and leaving me to hideous abandonment why don't you instead kill me? if you killed me," I plead sensibly, "I wouldn't feel the hideous abandonment. Just as when the most hideous of Berber chieftains takes a girl who's been masturbating to the point of blood and shoves a prick the size of a goat's into her as-yet-untouched-except-by-her-own-shit one-half-centimeter-diameter asshole and she doesn't say anything. She just looks at him. Then he turns her around on his cock. Just so: I want you to kill me so that there'll be no tomorrow."

he says, "OK I'll kill you."

I ask him how "I don't want anything too painful cause pain scares me."

"what do you care about pain when you don't care about death"

"that's not the point"

"what's the point?"

"there's no point to all this"

"then why do you want to die now?"

"cause I can remember pain but I can't remember death" he says convinced though it makes him feel good to hurt me, he cares enough about me to kill me and besides killing me'll be fun

it's good we always get along

now that I've got a daddy, life and death no longer matter

then the skin of his face looks like that of an old man because he's become a Nazi he has to be a Nazi now because he's German I'm a sailor his facial skin always becomes old when he's focused

And here it came to me on the path of sexuality . . . secretly . . . ambushing me . . . there was an infatuating warm smell coming from the bare skin, a soft lecherous cajolery. And yet there was something about it so solemn and compelling as to make one almost clap one's heart in awe.

"do you want to eat one last time?" as if I was really in front of a firing squad and being granted one last request so I asked the Nazi if I could smoke a cigarette, though I don't smoke cigarettes, rather than put one out on my body which I also swore, one day, if he really loved me, I'd do

then I said to the Nazi, "I'm hungry"

"that's because you're about to die a thing like that always makes a guy hungry all those Spanish anarchists were ravenous but they had the discipline not to say so they were sleepy too"

I protested to the Nazi I didn't want to fall asleep cause then I wouldn't know what it is to die and I had only one chance to die you only die for love once then I looked up to him and he was slightly taller than me and asked him what we should do now cause I didn't have any food in the house cause pirating took up too much of my time

"we don't have to do a fuckin' thing we don't we can do whatever we want" he puts thumbs on my throat my cock grows and rubs against his stomach

There was danger now . . . somewhere . . . lying in wait . . . not the open but an ambush . . . not what seemed to be here . . . something that would actually tear me, or the me that is memory, apart . . . This had hard corners and was tangible reality. My eyes awakened out of sleep.

"but do we have to stay here a long time" while I was still able to speak

his thumbs pressed down harder my cock got harder for his thumbs

After I died, the boxer bent down over me. A curve of an eyebrow was all that showed that he had feelings. My flesh was still warm. He lifted a sheet over me, then stretched himself out on top of me under the sheet. For the first time his undressed body was next to mine.

The boxer pressed his bulge into mine. Where mine used to be. Death desexualized. He kissed my forehead while his hard thing plowed exploring into my hole. I screamed from the pain deep inside me. He went wild shooting off into me. He hadn't done that before. He clutched at me, twisted my nipples, tore my face. The myth had become apparent. His fucking cock sounded an opening into my pubis's innominate bone.

I opened my eyes fully and saw the boxer standing on my right, wiping sperm off his cock. The wind from the open sea made both of us shiver. I managed to touch his mouth just as he lay down on me again and pushed his tongue through my closed mouth as no child has ever kissed. "I'm not going to leave you."

GLUTTONY

SARA MAITLAND

GLUTTONY

GLUTTONY

Classic Baked Apple
Ingredients: 4 large apples
8 tbsp jam
1 oz butter
4 tbsp sugar
4 tbsp castor sugar

1. Wash dry and core apples.
2. Place in a greased ovenproof dish and fill each apple with jam. Add a small knob of butter to each.
3. Put water in the bottom of dish then bake at 375°F (190°C) Gas 5 for 25 minutes. Serve sprinkled with sugar and cream if desired.

Of course I loved the baby. Of course I did. That was the point. It was because I loved the baby. My breasts would ache with loving that baby. Sometimes I would lie in the bath, soaking deep, deep in hot water, toe tips, tummy, nipples and neck — with head and curly hair looped up into an elastic band on the top — sticking out, like little pink coral islands in ocean of warmth. And I would soak there staring at the islands of my breasts, and watching that magical marbling of the water where the milk flowed invisibly out. Sweet fine food for my lovely milky baby.

Mother Angela, her skin as fine as tissue paper, her smile as bright as morning, places her almost transparent hand on her little novice's head. It is a touch gentle and loving, but it is also a judgement and a reprimand. Sister Juliana puts down the cup. She wants to say, "But Mother I am thirsty." Mother Angela knows that she wants to say so, and knows too that she herself wants to reply,

Child, so am I. I have been thirsty from matins until vespers for forty-two years, and I am still thirsty. Let us, just this once as no one is watching us, drink and drink; even plants need watering and so do we; let us let the cold sweet water dribble down our chins and cool our necks." And deep in her is again and still a sense of the profound unfairness of God. Their Blessed Sister Catherine in Siena, who was only a tertiary, who was not even a nun, was freed by Christ from hunger, she felt no hunger, she felt only repulsion. And yet she herself, fifty years on, would still wake in the night her stomach churning with hunger – not even for the exotic food of her noble childhood, but for something as simple as a little piece of bread, the piece her old nurse used to give her, broken in the morning from the end of the loaf, crusty and cool. And this little one, this secret favourite of all her novices, of all her daughters – what mother does not wish to nourish the child that comes to her in hunger and thirst? What mother does not desire to open her dress and let the little one suck and suck?

But Sister Juliana is not a child; Sister Juliana is not a baby. Sister Juliana, fifteen years old and beautiful, is a woman. The time has come for her to put away childish things. What Mother does not desire for her child the sight of the living God, the salvation prepared for her before the dawn of time, the robes of glory like a bride with which the angels will clothe her?

She says only, "Dear Sister, Christ thirsted on the cross and no one gave him fresh water, and yet he has promised that he will give you the water of life, and then you will never be thirsty again. Come." And she rests her ancient hand on Sister Juliana's arm, pretending to need support, and leads her away across the cloister, away from the well, away from temptation. Later she will speak to the Sisters in Chapter, speak with that sweetness and wit which have made her renowned, which bring Bishops and rulers to her cloister door seeking advice, which bring lovely children to the novitiate so that she will have to undertake the responsibility of seeing their tired and hungry faces in the refectory, of hearing the strange swish and thud sound that twenty women together taking the discipline in their cells make Friday after Friday. She is tired now herself, but later she will remind them that their brothers train themselves, discipline themselves and starve themselves just for the week of festival so that they can outrun one another in races and leap up the palazzo steps to claim their garlands and prizes. The Blessed Apostle Paul had told them they must run the race so as to win it; the garland that Christ will put on their heads will be of flowers that never fade, the prize will be the beauty of God's glory forever, the sweetness of his presence everlasting. They were God's athletes: would they be other than in training?

Oh I loved the baby. I know a lot of women who hate those night feeds, but not me; I remember those as peaceful and happy times. On the sofa in our living room, cushions piled around both of us, a throne of warmth and comfort, a book, a box of those wonderful dark Bentick chocolates, and the pale scrambled-egg coloured dawns, thickening visibly out of the grey times at the end of the darkness. And the autumn sun rising apricot gold and the baby, softly furred as a peach, warm as toast, buttery and cuddly, laid sweetly across my soft belly and sucking, sucking, sucking at my breasts. A land of milk and honey for my sweet child. Tiny joyful grunts and squeaks. My own little suckling pig with my apple in its mouth. Loved? I adored the baby. Don't look at me like that.

Anyway it isn't my fault. You can't understand. You never knew my mother. No, I'm not blaming her, I'm not saying a word against her, now or ever, but you do have to understand. She had a hard life, I mean a hard childhood. You look around you now, at the flat and at me and at Tony, and it is too easy to forget that we have done most of this ourselves. I'm not lazy, I have worked hard. Like my mother. She was born in 1922, in Sunderland, the oldest of six children; one a year for six years, they were good Catholics my grandparents. Her father worked in the docks, he was a good man, a good man and a good hard-working docker. I remember Pa — we all called him Pa; now Nan I don't remember, she died when I was little, I hardly ever saw her, Sunderland was a very long way from Bristol when I was growing up. But my mother remembered her, talked about her, made us know her —a big strong Wearside woman, and you had to be to bring six children through the depression, up there then.

When my mother was growing up there wasn't enough to eat. As simple as that. In 1934 my mother's little sister, the next one down from her, died. You can't say she died of starvation. My mother always said she died of the measles, but people don't die of the measles if they're well fed, if they're strong and healthy. I had the measles, I expect you had the measles, everyone has the measles. Well my would-have-been aunt died of the measles when my mother was twelve years old. That's bound to affect someone, isn't it? No, I don't blame her. I'm just trying to explain.

She did well in school, all things considered, and Pa and Nan supported her in that. She got to the grammar school, and they were proud of her — sturdy Geordie Labour Party they were both of them, and they believed in education, even for the girls. My mother always said she would have gone into local government, as a secretary, been a Civil Servant, something like that, a long way up for a docker's daughter in the 30s. Then the war came. My mother had a "good war" as it's called. She was sent to India. She loved it — well it wasn't Tyne and Wear in the Depression for one thing. She got promoted and she ended up a sergeant. She liked India too, it was hot and colourful; when she talked about it you could always see her glow a bit. She was demobilized in 1946. She once told me she was scared then; scared to go back home to all that poverty and waste and greyness and the outside loo. She met my father in London on her de-mob leave, and they got married six months later. He was a school teacher and became headmaster of a small primary school in Bristol. It was a long way up and a long way away from the Sunderland docks. It was the 1950s, the "you've never had it so good" years, and for her that was true. She had me in 1950 and my sister in 1953 and my little brother in 1958. She was happy, fulfilled and contented, but she didn't forget anything. When I was two I won a "bouncing baby" competition. She was so proud. She kept that photograph of sweet chubby me and a huge cup right out on the front room mantelpiece. And I know why: she could feed her children. She loved to feed us. She used to bake us biscuits. I'd come in from school and there would be this warm rich smell; little round hot biscuits with crunchy brown sugar on top. And cinnamon toast, nursery toast we used to call it; even now the smell of hot cinnamon and butter makes me drool. Sunday lunch, shoulder of lamb and gravy, roast potatoes, little and crispy, and then baked apples with cloves stuck in and custard, or apple crumble. Those sorts of things. Roast chicken with little bacon rolls on your birthday, and mashed potatoes silky smooth and suet pudding with golden syrup on the top sinking in and trickling down the sides like those little hill villages in Umbria, and pork chops, and something called cheese dreams, we used to have them for tea on Sundays, baked slowly in the oven, the only meal in the world that justifies those dreadful Kraft processed cheese slices, and you can't make them right with anything else.

She was immensely understanding. Later on, when I was about ten or twelve I suppose, I started doing something that was really quite naughty; if my father had known he would have half-killed me I expect: though talking it over now with friends I think that almost all children do it at some time or another — I used to take money from her purse, or steal small change if she sent me on errands. I used to buy cream buns from the baker: doughnuts stuffed with that fake cream which now I couldn't swallow if I had to. I don't know why; it wasn't hunger, it was the utter delightful wickedness of it I think. Hiding round the back until you had finished, wiping your mouth very very carefully, checking your front for crumbs — they were the best tasting doughnuts I have ever sampled. The point is that my mother knew — she told me so years later — and decided to let me keep my secret. She never said a word. I think she was proud in a way that she had enough money for it not to be a disaster if her children nicked the odd small change, but I think more than that she understood, understood wisely and deeply the need for secrecy, the need for secret feeding and special treats. It was love for her and it was food and she was happy, and so were we.

Krapfen
Ingredients: 2 eggs
3 fl oz beer
4 oz plain flour
pinch of salt
1½ lb dessert apples
oil for frying
sugar and cinnamon

1. Separate eggs. Beat yolks, beer, flour and salt to a smooth batter. In another bowl beat the egg whites till stiff then fold into the batter.
2. Peel and grate the apples, then mix into the batter.
3. Heat the oil for frying to 360°F (180°C) in a deep fryer.
4. Slide spoonfuls of the apples and batter mixture into the hot oil and fry for about 2 minutes, or until crisp.
5. When cooked remove from pan on slotted spoon, drain well. roll krapfen in castor sugar and cinnamon mixed. Serve hot.

In her stall in the dim chapel Mother Angela excoriates herself for the sin of envy; her conscience scalds her. Deep under the folds of her habit her hands twitch distressfully. She stills them, but she cannot still either her envy or her conscience. Who is she to envy the graces that God sees fit to offer the deserving? Who is she to envy Sister Catherine the peace of not feeling hunger. God does with each soul what is proper for it. Who is she to question that the hunger, the daily suffering from it, is not itself a grace from God, allowing her to be ever more united with the suffering humanity of her saviour on the cross. She does not, she tells herself sternly, she does not need ecstacy, she does not need visions, God has dealt graciously with her. She needs no spiritual gymnastics when daily, daily, she can receive the physical humanity of God in the Sacrament.

Yet I, least of all souls,
Take Him in my hand.
Eat Him and drink Him
And do with Him what I will.
Why then should I trouble myself
As to what the angels experience?

Not her own words, alas, even that joy she has never been given. No joys, no graces, no ecstatic visions, no angelic experiences. Just a long, long life. "Take me home," she wants to demand of her God, she has after all demanded more of Kings. She banishes the thought. Her nagging hunger replaces it. Under her habit her hands clench suddenly in an attack of physical rage, that fades almost immediately into irritation and then guilt.

For god's sake don't look at me like that. If there's one thing I can't stand it's that sort of puritanism about food. I can't abide it. It's bloody unfeminist as well. There's no morality in skinniness you know. Fat is a feminist issue. I'm not going to reconstruct my whole body to give pleasure to some dictatorial fashion bosses. Tony isn't complaining. Wasn't. He liked it. It's not as though I was obese; well . . . well I admit at the moment that I'm not in great shape, but I did have a baby less than six months ago you know. I can take it off any time I want to. It's interesting how deep that dualism goes, isn't it? That real hatred of the body and the flesh; the more the worse. Funny that the '60s set sex free for those who want it; now if you're not fucking like a bunny rabbit you must be neurotic, but food goes on being wicked, yes wicked. Naughty but nice. There's nothing wrong with a little bit of hedonism. Pleasure is an important principle. Look at all those poor little kids with anorexia and bulimia and all those other eating disorders — it is exactly, it's exactly that expression of yours that has done that to them. Yes I feel guilty, of course I bloody feel guilty, but I hope you do too.

Oh God . . .

Alright if I'm honest I have to admit that the whole thing was getting out of control, I mean years ago.

I'll tell you a story. We laugh about it quite often, me and my friends, Tony and others. Well, we used to; I don't suppose anyone will laugh about it again. When I was an undergraduate I went on a holiday to Italy — to Tuscany and Umbria mostly, we toured around a lot. It was great fun. We had this little battered car and there were four of us and we travelled about, just looking and enjoying; sitting in bar-cafés and drinking cappuccini and eating those wonderful little sweet pastries, and fruit, and big rough bowls of wonderful pasta. What's your favourite? Mine's cappelletti in brodo I think; when that ricotta and spinach stuffing sort of explodes into your mouth. And the sun hot, hot, hot and those wonderful peaches. In Venice they have little blood oranges and in Florence that unbelievable gelato limone that you can just buy from quite ordinary ice-cream stands in the street. And I still say that when it comes to cheap wine — I'm not talking about real claret or anything, I just mean plonk, that there is nothing to touch some of those rural white wines from central Italy. Good imported Orvieto, secco of course, isn't bad at the moment, but it doesn't have that almost flowery taste that you can get if you're lucky in some little taverna off the main road, and you can sit in the shade all afternoon, and drink and eat those stunning great fat peaches, all dribbly until the wasps come. And that was the first time I'd ever been. We go most years now of course, Tony and I. It was the first time and I was overwhelmed by it, even though I didn't really know then what to look for and often would take the menu turistico and look round at local people and wonder how you could order the things they were eating. Zucchini flowers for instance: you know, you'd see them in the greengrocers and think "how odd". When someone showed me how to dip them in flour and deep fry them I thought I had learned what the angels eat in heaven.

Anyway there we were, and the people I was with were lovely and we had a lot of fun. But the point is, we went one day to Gubbio, which — and I've been back so I know — is the most enchanting town. Very dark and troubled under its mountain. Well we arrived in Gubbio at about mid morning, and then we split up. Different people wanted to do different things — they make nice pottery there and Clare wanted to look for some and there are a couple of museums and the cathedral right at the top. When we got back at the appointed hour, the other three were all full of their cultural delights and they asked me what I had been doing and it turned out that I had spent the whole two hours looking for a restaurant for us to have lunch in. I had inspected every damn eating place in the town I should think, for money value and for food value. It was mean of them to laugh, because they liked the food too: I had found a gem, where we had some cold veal with cream and caper sauce. I can still remember, and they appreciated it. But they always laugh about it now and call me the woman who prefers menus to the renaissance.

It isn't fair really, because they all like coming to dinner still, and I cook better than almost anyone I know. Clare came only a month or so ago, to meet the baby. She's one of those people that when you go to dinner there you arrive at eight and you know she hasn't even started cooking, she may not even have decided what she's going to cook and she laughs and calls it pot luck, and then everyone has to drink for hours while she messes about; and by then you're too drunk to enjoy it, even if it were to be enjoyable food which it usually isn't. I do think that is rude. It seems to me that if you ask people to eat with you you do owe them something half-way decent. And when she comes here she eats like a pig. It's alright for them to be so high-minded about a bit of Italian culture, but she never turns down decent food if someone else will make it for her. Speaking of which, would you like something to eat? I've got some quite OK apple cake in the kitchen.   Alright. You think this is bad taste don't you. What do you expect me to do? Starve myself to death? It's not just my fault. It's not just my fault. I'm sorry. Ohh . . . oh God. Oh God . . .

Hot apple flan with calvados
Ingredients: 8 oz sweet flan pastry as preferred
              1½ lbs cooking apples
              2 oz butter
              5 oz icing sugar
              3 tbsp calvados

1. Bake pastry blind in 8-inch flan ring.
2. While pastry is cooking, peel and core apples, and cut into quarters or eighths depending on size.
3. Melt butter in saucepan, add apples and cook over high heat until they are light brown.
4. Add 4 oz icing sugar and 2 tbsp calvados and cook gently until apples are tender.
5. Spoon apples and some of the juice into the warm cooked flan case. Sprinkle sieved icing sugar over and place in warm oven until needed.
6. To serve: warm remaining calvados in a ladle. Light and pour over flan immediately. Take, flaming, to table, and serve with whipped cream.

Weariness, for Mother Angela, is one more thing that must be put aside. She rises from her stall and goes to the refectory. Her daughters rise and bow. She takes her place and sings a blessing. In front of each sister there is a small cube of bread, and a glass of water. The water is drawn at dawn and set in the sun; now it is

warm and a little dusty. In a row along the centre of the table are
set bowls of olives. They have been there for several days and their
skins are shrivelling. Every sister is free to eat them: very few of
them do. Mother Angela observes them with pleasure, her huge
shining eyes full of love and holiness. She notices that Sister Maria
is crumbling her bread needlessly; later Mother Angela will tell her
that it is as much a discipline to eat what you are given as it is to
fast. Christ gives them himself in the form of bread, bread is
sacred, not to be sprinkled under the table secretly, but eaten and
rejoiced in. Did they not come to this place to imitate the poverty of
Christ: the poor do not scatter good bread on the floor. Sister
Maria will be sulky, as she too often is, but Mother Angela wants
no hysterical excitement in her house; no manifestations of the
miraculous, and no dying young women, she has seen that too
often and loves them all too much. She wants love and prayer,
prayer and love: when Sister Maria learns to smile Mother Angela
will let her fast further. She looks down at her own cube of bread
and takes a hold of herself so that she does not cram it into her
mouth, salivating and munching, but treats it as the holy thing it
is. There must be courtesy here at the bare table, courtesy greater
than that displayed in the Courts of Princes, out of respect for the
bread, out of love for the giver and out of charity for the
company. But she is so hungry. And when she is hungry the bread
tastes so sweet; she tries to hold it in her mouth to prolong her
pleasure, but her throat and stomach demand it. She swallows
and rejoices. She overcomes a spontaneous desire to help herself
to one of the olives. She imagines the moment of stillness that
would descend on the refectory if she were to do so, and she
laughs internally.

I got my degree in 1972. And you remember how exciting
everything was then. There was feminism, which was and still is
immensely important to me, I felt we were on the edge of
something huge and real; the old standards were being desecrated

and profaned. I gave up being a Catholic, I stripped myself of all those old guilts, it seemed summer all the time and I was very happy. I went to London and started working for a libertarian magazine; I wanted to be a political journalist then, but for various reasons I started doing a series of restaurant reviews for them — kind of adding it on to my editorial duties; it was rather fun and there were lots of new places opening up and lots of old places that people hadn't heard of. And I was good at it. Then we added a cooking column, it was meant to be magically radical somehow: how to put hash into chocolate-chip cookies and where to find free-range eggs, but I started to believe then, what I certainly believe now: that a great deal too much fuss has been made about those sorts of things, and that the most radical thing you can do around food issues is to enjoy things. More and more my column was about enjoying cooking, enjoying food. You can make wonderful meals very cheaply if you want to, if you bother to think about it.

It's not just conspicuous consumption you know. In the early seventies there was a great deal of puritanism about those sorts of things, but the women's movement has grown up now. We used to be so stern with each other, all that endless brown rice and lentils — though actually you can do some pretty neat things with lentils if you put your mind to it, but you know what I mean. So when I was offered the job at "You and Yours" I jumped at it. Some people were a bit dubious — it is after all hardly a hotbed of the revolution, but I thought that it was important that women did get those big jobs, I didn't want to be part of a ghetto, I wanted to take feminism into the real world: no one bitched when other women went to work for the *Guardian* and so on. It is true that the sort of writing I do now is rather more gourmet, but we've all grown up and got richer, and despite all the mockery I don't see anything much wrong with being a foodie. And the Television programme was a lot of fun you have to admit. The job I liked best of all actually was the time I spent with the supermarket chain, introducing women — via those little cards — to things they wouldn't have known how to cook before.

And then I met Tony, and fell in love. Yes, he is very rich, and of course I like that, I'm not going to pretend I don't. Wouldn't you? Are you jealous? And he is an old Tory. But, well you can't control love can you, and he certainly doesn't bully me. I mean I haven't changed my politics because of him. Oh for God's sake; yes, it is true I voted SDP. I'm sick and tired of the Labour Party if you really want to know — what real support has it ever given to women?

Look do you want me to tell you about the baby or not? OK. I got pregnant. I was really pleased, I was so happy I can't even tell you. I was over the moon. You know how it feels, something valuable and special tucked inside you, growing there, filling you up, ripening secretly. My truffle, I used to think, my precious underground peanut. You know. When the baby moved I could feel it like a fish; my lovely troutling I would sing to my stomach. There was the baby rising perfectly like a soufflé: I have some really pretty Edwardian soufflé dishes, individual soufflé dishes, you know the little ones with sides a bit higher than ramekins; they are fluted and hand-painted, with gilded rims. They are rather valuable and very beautiful — and that was what I felt like. I read somewhere that when West Indian teenagers go out all dressed up and walk in that lordy way they have down the streets, showing off, they call it "strutting your stuff", well when I was pregnant I wanted to strut my stuff all round the world, and at the same time it was secret and dark in there where I was cooking up my delicious baby: it used to make me laugh, just thinking that happy thought. You know when a soufflé is cooking you aren't meant to crash things around, and you aren't meant to look in the oven. Actually that's a bit of a myth now because with thermostat-controlled ovens the whole soufflé business is a doddle — but so is pregnancy, or it was for me so perhaps the analogy holds. When I had my amniocentesis they said they could tell me what sex the baby was going to be but I did not want to know — I felt it would be like peeking at a soufflé rather than waiting just longer than you think you should, and then snatching it out with the top edges just splitting open and browning perfectly and everyone saying "ooh" and "ahhh" and "oh, aren't you clever?" and that extraordinary mixture of sweet and savoury that a good dessert soufflé gives you; it's one of the few very hot things that really do melt in the mouth.

In fact I cooked quite a lot of soufflés while I was expecting the baby. They were wonderful to eat, light and nourishing and fun and I had this little private joke about being a soufflé dish which made me giggle more and more as my tummy swelled.

And the birth was good too. Not quick or easy particularly, but emotionally rich, darker than I had expected. But down there in the depths of the darkness there is a great rich place, tasting of chocolate fudge cake, a warm place in the bottom of the pain. Tony was wonderful. He was simply there for me, and also there between me and the world, so that no one could interfere with that dark rich centre. I had not expected it quite honestly, not expected to be given so much of him. He had remembered everything, Buxton water on a sponge to suck, ice in a tidy thermos, and afterwards, before the slightly shocked eyes of the midwife and doctor, he stood there in the labour ward and mixed the best Bloody Mary I have ever tasted, and abracadabra out of his brief-case like a conjuror he produced pâté de foie gras and little biscuits and made the hospital people eat them with us, and then strawberries in a real punnet instead of a plastic container. The two of us were laughing, and the baby so perfectly sweet and delightful was sucking and sleeping. Oh I was so happy.

Mother Angela goes to her cell, still biting down on her hunger and tiredness, still full of rejoicing. Of one thing at least she is certain and that is that God prefers a loving heart to a bleeding back. Christ's back bled and his hands and feet and side were pierced because he loved us. Not to force himself into love, but because he already loved. Love first, then the disciplines of loving. Just training, she tells herself, as she has told three generations of novices. Just sharing with him what he shared with us. In unity. In unity, she murmurs. If you do not love the body there is no purpose to disciplining it. When we learn to read, held in our mother's arms, taken from our toys, we do not imagine that we hate the intelligence, but we must train it, train it. When we struggle out of bed to pray we do not imagine that we hate the soul, no we love the soul and train it up the way it, of its true nature, desires to go. We have been given a way, we may unite ourselves with God, through discipline. Surely it is worth it. That it works she has no doubt; she has not doubted since that strange spring forty years ago when she and Francis had been tempted, when she had been overwhelmed with desire, when her body made its own demands although her head and her heart and her spirit had no desire to leave her lovely convent, the sweet company of her sisters, to bring on him and herself both shame and unhappiness. But she had learned, as the little novices learn now, to subdue the flesh, to keep it in its place, and now she is old and honoured and happy.

She is trying, she realizes, to persuade herself; to silence the other self who says you are over seventy years old and you have earned a rest. One olive cannot do an old lady any harm. The olives will still be sitting on the table, one shrivelled olive, not even especially sweet, just one. She wavers. Then she lies down on her pallet. "Get thee behind me Satan," she says and fixes her eyes on the image of Mary holding the sweet child. She gives thanks that she has resisted the temptation to eat, even though she cannot believe that Mary will appreciate how real the temptation is. She lies quietly waiting for sleep.

Mary says to her quite clearly and not in the ears of her mind, not in the ears of her flesh, Mary says, "Dear Child, you have nourished so many; now nourish my son." And Mary places the infant Jesus in Mother Angela's arms. It is over fifty years since Mother Angela has held a baby, and she takes the Christ Child tentatively, but her breasts, her ancient saggy breasts with nipples as wrinkled as the olives, respond, and his warm sleepy little hand curves up, petting her. Milk and love flow from her into him, and she can scarcely bear the happiness he gives her. She feeds him for a while until he seems to sleep and then, with a gracious word of thanks, she returns him to his mother. She is weeping with delight and humility, almost she wonders whether Mary can really know of her weakness and her temptation. She is not worthy. Mary says, "There is no worthiness, but that God has called you worthy." The two women smile over the sleeping baby.

And then with a trumpet blast and surrounded by angels, the great Ruler of the Creation comes to her; the five wounds glow with fire and the whole universe is a tiny jewel in his crown. "Blessed," sing the angels, "blessed are they who hunger and thirst after righteousness for they shall be satisfied." And he takes her in the power of his arms and opens the dazzling raiment and feeds her at his breast and the milk is sweeter than wine and smells of distant honey. The angels sing, "Oh taste and see the sweetness of the Lord," and she suckles and suckles, a little child again in the arms of love, a young woman again in the arms of her lover, an old old lady who had not dared to hope to be given such glory.

Alsatian apple tart

Ingredients:	Pastry	Filling
	8 oz plain flour	4 golden delicious apples
	4 oz butter	2½ oz castor sugar
	2 tbsp castor sugar	½ pint double cream
	1 egg	2 eggs
	white wine to mix	2 oz vanilla sugar
		1 lemon

1. Mix pastry and cool for 30 mins. Then roll on lightly floured surface to line 9-inch flan dish. Bake blind at 400°F (200°C) Gas 6 for 20 minutes.
2. Peel apples, cut in half and remove cores. Arrange on

pastry, round side up; sprinkle lightly with sugar and bake for 10 minutes.

3. Meanwhile, whip cream and beat in eggs, vanilla sugar, grated rind of lemon and castor sugar until creamy. Spread creamed mixture over apples. Reduce heat to 350°F (180°C) Gas 4 and cook tart for 20 minutes. Serve warm.

Yes, I am getting to the point. I'm trying to anyway. It is hard to talk about the baby. She was completely lovely. She was so soft and dimpled and silly and funny and loving and warm and strong and sweet. She was almost totally bald when she was born but her ears had a fringe of adorable fair hair along the top of them, like a pixie, surprisingly long. If you held her up to the sunlight her ears would glow pink and her ear-fringe would shine like spun gold. It made Tony and me giggle.

And then one night I got up to feed her. She was crying so I got up to feed her. When I went to her crib she was yelling but as soon as she saw me she smiled, a great wide welcoming grin and immediately I was happy to be up with her, and I carried her into the living room and fed her. She sucked and sucked, and I smiled and teased her, called her a greedy little thing, but gently, and night was thinning out into morning, and when she had finished and dozed off, I was ravenously hungry. I shifted her onto my shoulder and went into the kitchen to find somethng to eat and there was practically nothing; certainly nothing you could prepare one-handed with a baby on your shoulder. No, not nothing, I had forgotten. There was a small piece of dolcelatte. I remember now, because I looked at it and thought how like my breast it was, soft and creamy with those delicate veins. And I ate it and I was still famished, starving and a bit cross with Tony for being so selfish and eating all the left-overs even the ginger biscuits. I thought I would put the baby back to bed and then cook something. I carried her into her room and started to change her nappy. She was still pretty much asleep, with her arms tucked in close against her body, so I didn't put the ceiling light on, just the soft glow from the night light. She was wearing one of those sleep suits that you are supposed to be able to change a nappy without taking off, but it was soaking. I was irritated and I almost didn't bother; you can just slip a clean nappy on and let it go if you want to. I wish I had. But I wanted her to sleep comfortably, so that I could too later in the morning when I was full of whatever it was I was going to cook myself. So I stripped her right off, even her vest once I had got started; she had those little vests that cross over and tie in the front because she never seemed to like having things pulled over her head. And then she was naked and sleepy and fat and sweet and I was tired and hungry and I reached for a clean vest and she rolled over and there was her beautiful little rump stuck up in the air and those wonderful ears just catching the gentle light, and I knew exactly what I was doing and I knew I shouldn't and I couldn't resist it. It was as simple as that, I couldn't resist it. Just one bite I said to myself, one bite won't hurt her. She tasted heavenly. After the first bite I couldn't stop. A delicate cross between chicken and veal I would say; I thought of salt and perhaps paprika, but I didn't have them to hand, and I couldn't stop to go and get them. I ate my baby, à la tartare. It was the best meal I had ever had. Simply delicious. I loved her. I loved her and I ate her.

After considerable thought, and consultation with her confessor, Mother Angela told no one of the gift she had been given. She wanted no hysterical excitements and manifestations of the miraculous in her house. Nor does she want her daughters to grow up believing that penance and training and love are in order to gain spiritual prowess. But she was contented. Even when the glorious vision faded she was left with another, a lighter gift, and as she goes about her convent, from dim chapel to bright garden, from austere cell to airy refectory, over and over again she sees Eve pause.

Eve must have paused just before she bit into the apple, either then or just before she plucked it from the tree. She paused, but this was Eden, this was the original sinless apple, round and smooth and smelling of the first long perfect summer in all creation. She was overwhelmed with longing. She ate the apple. Genesis got it wrong. It wasn't pride, it wasn't desire for knowledge, it wasn't even competition with God. It was greed. The apple beguiled her and she ate.

So though Mother Angela's skin is finer than tissue paper, her smile is far brighter than the morning, and she goes on her way rejoicing.

This story comes with special thanks to Ros Hunt who helped me with the theology and Carol Fry who helped me with the cookery.

ENVY

LESLIE DICK

ENVY

ENVY

PRELUDE

It was heaven. The skies were very clear and high, with light clouds scudding across them in high wind, wind that took the form of easy breezes down below. The garden was perfectly landscaped, an ideal balance of cultivation and nature, with wayward paths chancing upon carefully composed views, and the soothing sound of running water, the endless twisting brooks and gentle fountains combining with the distant birdsong to make a natural muzak. The sun fell between the shadowy leaves as we walked, our feet barely touching the damp path, as we floated through paradise, discussing the pros and cons of existence.

I remember Corinne still retained traces of the vehemence, the emotional vehemence that is characteristic of the sublunary sphere. This had the real charm of novelty, for me especially, since I'd avoided the place for so long. It was fading fast, however, gleaming out like sun reflected off a shadowy mirror, a mirror already draped with heavy cloth of gold. Corinne still gleamed, and I walked with her to catch those gleams, and argue through again the oldest conversation, to be or not to be.

Of course she, Corinne, desperately wanted another go. This had all the naïve charm of a puppy or a kitten chasing a ping-pong ball. After a few runs through the mill, most of us are extremely satisfied by things here, reading, walking, enjoying all the things that the specific vehemence of emotion precludes down there. As she spoke, it came back to me, how one could be walking through sublunary gardens, as beautiful as this one (though not so extensive and infinitely varied, of course), and one would be concentrating on a broken heart, some loss or another, tied to a cramp, an ache, an obsession, and the loveliness of the garden would come through in snatches, glimpses, but mostly it merely performed the function of a backdrop to an emotional drama.

What we give up, when we choose to stay here, is desire. And it's not a struggle, we've been through the struggle by then, and we're out the other side. We're quite happy to stumble on melons eternally.

But Corinne, the puppy, wasn't. She wanted to go back. I found it delightful.

"But it's such a lottery, my dear, *who* you get. I mean, you can't *choose*. Not like in the movies, remember that marvellous Hollywood thing with the little girl who *chose* her parents?"

"Yes, they tried to talk her out of it, as well — they said the couple wasn't worth gracing with her presence."

"Well that's not what I'm saying, sweetheart. I'm just trying to make out why it is that you want to leave . . ."

"Because I *like* it, I like the vehemence that you've let go, sliding out of it like an overcoat slipping off. I want to wear the overcoat, and walk down noisy streets. I want to take my chances. I want to fall in love."

"It all begins with being a baby, being one thing to one woman, and that love then is where you fall. You never get over that one, you know. Everything later is just a pale shadow of that first substance, an attempt to compensate for that first, inevitable loss —"

"But that's what's so fascinating — I mean, I know you don't know anything about it at the time . . ."

A bird of paradise in all its bright plumage flew past, and we paused, to take a breath and watch.

"But I like the process of attachment, I like the way presence and absence make everything up for the baby: language, skin, bodies — existence *is* that oscillation of attachment and separation."

"Not everyone would agree with you there. . ."

"It feels like an ocean, I want to swim in it."

"There are some very nice beaches here, you know."

"I know."

"It's the suffering, and the endless *changing,* and the terrible *confusion* that I'm so happy without. I like this clarity, but then I suppose I had my fill of confusion."

"I *have* chosen my parents anyway."

"*What?*"

"Well I'm working on it."

"You must be joking, that's a fundamental rule of existence —it's arbitrary."

"Well, not completely. Not completely arbitrary. I mean, there's all the genetic stuff . . ."

"But that's just the existential necessities, hard facts like weather or geography."

"*Angels* are allowed to make specific interventions."

"That's not your sphere. You're *not* an angel. You're just — what do they call it — you're just a ghost."

"Don't be horrible to me."

"I'm sorry, Corinne. But this really is unheard of."

"I'm setting a precedent. I'm working on it."

"And they're taking this seriously?"

"I've been listening in. And I've been *dreaming* —"

"I had no idea."

"— and I know where I want to go."

"I should have guessed. I should have distracted you. I thought your attraction to that place was *sweet.* Now I realize it's more like an obsession."

"But I'm persuading them. It's specific, and justified, and also something of an experiment."

"OK, tell me about it . . ."

"In this dream, I was a woman . . ."

CHLAMYDIA

Everyone was reproducing, suddenly. The magazines named "a baby" as the fashionable accessory of 1988. Jeanie realized she'd been avoiding friends with babies, doubled over inside with the intensity of her feeling. She was like a miser who cannot bear to visit someone who ostentatiously displays their wealth. The extremity of her desire for a child was a dark, heart-clenching secret, and though she joked about it, no one knew how completely it had come to shape her days. By making jokes, she deflected attention, even her own attention, from the agonizing exigencies of her wish.

And, she thought, maybe it's true, that wanting is just an endless series, that once you get *a*, you long for *b*, and once *b* dissolves in the mists of time, *c* looms over the horizon, all holding out that same crazed promise: some kind of relation, contact, collision with some other, something *else*.

Jeanie found herself imagining the body of a child, as she walked down the street, on everyday expeditions, to the super-market, the dry cleaner. The soft skin, round arms, kicking legs of a baby came to mind, in the ordinary reverie of everyday. In bed, lying against Stephen, she pictured herself, sculptured herself into an eight-year-old, fitting so easily into the shape made by his sleepy body. In imagination, she became smaller, and Stephen like a great green hill, or large animal, that, childish, she could curl up against. She imagined lifting up a two-year-old, a three-year-old, standing holding the child on her right hip, supporting it with her arm, easily, easily, and laughing easily with another woman, standing, holding a kid on her hip. (She never imagined breastfeeding a baby, as if that would be going too far, indulging herself too much.) She could place herself in the kitchen, in imagination, and have a kid walk in, from school maybe. She could hold a baby in her two hands, against her shoulder, the baby's face next to her neck.

There were more and more women friends with babies now,

more and more people to avoid. It was just as she'd always predicted, as they hit thirty-three, thirty-four, thirty-five, they reproduced. She couldn't bear to see them. She avoided them. She dreamed constantly of having a baby and something going terribly wrong.

With their children on their laps, young mothers would advise against it. Wait a little longer, they said, it's really hard work. They'd insist how impossible her present way of life would become: no more restaurants, travelling, no more going out. She met friends whose twelve-week-old baby had never slept more than a couple of hours at a time. They looked haggard, traumatized. They looked like they were having a nervous breakdown. Jeanie listened as Simon spoke of the intransigence of his tiny son, his sense of horror at the intensity of the baby's demand, the baby's body twisting, straining furiously in his arms, screaming blue murder. The young man with his exhausted eyes told her his baby son was a monster.

Jeanie thought of a baby as something that would give her exactly what she had to have, precisely meet her needs. Her wish had all the urgency and thrill of unrequited love. And she went through all the usual things, the familiar routines of mistaken love: enraged frustration (*why* can't I have it?), unreal expectation (...and we would love each other for ever and ever, endlessly ...), fantasies of physical intimacy so vivid as to be hallucinatory (... the back of your neck, pale eyes looking, wet mouth ...).

Freud is quite explicit: the only thing that can possibly *really* give satisfaction to a woman, castrata, is the baby she produces, the baby that represents the phallus, represents her desire. In theory. In practice a baby keeps you up all night until you can't think, or work. Jeanie read in the paper, the women's page, how reading a book uninterrupted becomes a forgotten luxury. This meant everything and nothing to her, wanting as she did the total transformation of herself that she imagined giving birth would bring, and believing at the same time that the specific pleasures of solitude were something she couldn't do without.

Jeanie pictured her mother surrounded by kids, on a beach, with Jeanie herself as a child, Jeanie's sisters. Her mother was so pretty, with her "great legs", in shorts, sitting on the sandy beach, the sun pale yellow everywhere, and the kids, five-year-olds, three-year-olds, playing in the sand, with the small long waves, coming in. Like a snapshot, it was the fifties beach scene. Her mother calling out, to put some more nosecote on her nose. Standing still, the tedium of sun lotion. Rubbing sun block onto naked shoulders and back of the five-year-old girl, a floppy white sunhat and red bathing suit, cotton with small white flowers, a plastic spade in her fist. Her mother was younger, then, than Jeanie, now — in this scene, where kids wandered off and came back, her mother talking so eaily, laughing as she sits on the beach towel, her legs making triangles before her, sunglasses on, laughing with another woman lying beside her.

What was so terrible about these daydreams, what upset Jeanie so much, was the way they came unbidden, uncalled for. It was as if her desire came to her, welling up from inside; she had not given herself permission to want this. Something between a memory and a fantasy, her wish was painful, bringing tears as it rose up from the depths. She could play all the parts in these scenes: the child standing still, reluctantly (stand still, just for a minute, while I put this on), looking out across the sand, to the small waves, and then the mother, rubbing sun lotion over the child's back, her little shoulder blades and sweet neck in the shadow of the white cotton hat. Jeanie could be in both these bodies, and be the camera, circling around them, taking in the surroundings, the constant swish of waves breaking, the sense of wet sand giving under bare feet. She could pan across the beach, close-up on the child's neck (mother's p.o.v.), stare out towards the other kids digging in the wet sand (kid's p.o.v.), Jeanie could make the whole thing up, against her will.

Sometimes it seemed that envy divided the world up for her, into men and women. Men she despised, and pursued. Women she adored, they had a reality that men lacked, it was women who counted, so to speak, yet everything she did was a repudiation of the pleasures of femininity. She excluded herself from the secret life of the harem, that easy, laughing world of women and children. This is not for you, she felt. Jeanie built high walls, and planted trees and lawns, made a sunny beach, to put her imaginary women in — a grove of trees with oranges and lemons, flowers, birds — she put them there, like playing with dolls, she placed them in the garden, laughing easily, and built high walls, and locked herself out. It didn't matter that she knew this heavenly garden existed only in her imagination. This was the place she couldn't go, and as such it was very important to her.

So she used these images to draw boundaries, clean lines through the world: men wore suits, made money, pursuing empty goals, unable to make connections. Women wove webs of relation, an arm around a sleepy child. She placed herself outside both these realms, over here, where we undo family ties, mistrust longing, repudiate dependency, and stand alone. Over here, with the other oddballs. We cook when we please, and sleep badly. We fall in love relentlessly. We know the inside of the clinics well, the different illnesses we are particularly prone to: the infections, viruses, and unwanted pregnancies of this solitary life. Romance, romance: the shine on the nose, that gleam of glamour putting an edge on everything. I can picture myself with a hard edge, in my black overcoat, white face, red lipstick, in the cold city street. Where does this picture come from? Fashion photographs? A set of fictions: on my right, the harem garden I name paradise, forever excluding me; on my left, the businessmen in their dark-grey suits, and here, before me, the woman imagining herself being seen, the hard edge of a black coat against the noisy city.

These were the cards she'd dealt herself, glossy and flat, a set of impenetrable fictions with almost no connection to anything else

or anyone — Jeanie played out her cards, occasionally jostled by
another, like someone accidentally bumping into you in the
street, an unexpected touch you can neither anticipate nor
control. Occasionally jostled by some fragment of real life, she
continued to pore over her cards, turning them in sequence, like
a tarot reader for whom the images have taken on all the intensity
of real life.

Tuesday: *On the phone. Bette and Jeanie talked on the phone a
lot.*

J : I think about it all the time, *dream* about babies —

B : Really?

J : All the time. It's an obsession. Endlessly thinking about
what you can't have or don't have, or might have —

B : It's like a fantasy boyfriend, you can imagine everything
being so great —

J : Yes, it's a boyfriend-in-fantasy when you're twenty-five, and
a baby-in-fantasy when you're thirty-five — what you
haven't got. And then I guess it's also about the future,
right, a metaphor of our love for each other extending
indefinitely, our *attachment.*

B : Since you won't get married.

J : Yes, it's the only way to *say,* let's stick together for the
unforeseeable future. Saying let's have a baby is just a way
to say I do love you, really I do.

B : So actually having a baby would be a mistake.

J : I don't know. In this dream I had a baby and I didn't know
if it was a boy or a girl, it had no name. It's as if I'd
forgotten. This was *terrible.*

B : Mmm.

J : And there was another dream in which I had a baby and I
put it in the airing cupboard, to keep warm, but I forgot
about it, I went out, and while I was out I suddenly

remembered the baby and I was sure it was dead by now.

B : Wow. You have *lots* of these dreams?

J : Yup.

B : But they're all about neglecting the baby, forgetting about it. Maybe it's not a baby at all, maybe it's (what they call) *part* of you . . .

J : Oh yeah — my analyst always used to say, *part* of you, and I'd think, my left ear . . .

B : So what's suffocating in the airing cupboard? Your work?

J : Obviously my work. It goes without saying my work. It's all this flight from femininity lark, this — can't be a man, won't be a woman routine.

B : Are there other dreams?

J : I always forget the best ones.

Monday: *On the phone.*

J : I think I've got this problem with my sister, you know, she's got the babies, I get the books. Like you *can't* have both.

B : It's like Connie and Isabel, division of labour, they couldn't both wear jeans, even.

J : When I have long hair, Louise has short hair, and vice versa. Always.

B : When Isabel sold her car, Connie finally learned to drive.

J : Are we so envious, so scared of taking things away from each other?

B : It's being scared of being too alike, it's identifying so much that you have to go to incredible lengths to distinguish yourself, to make sure you're not one and the same.

J : But are we scared of obliterating or being obliterated! It's like feeling, it could've been *me*. You look at — I look at my sister, and I feel, that's me, *but*.

B : So what's stopping you?

J : I don't know, I mean, I'm the girl who has abortions, right, not the one with the sweet little offspring in the pram.

B : Humph.

J : And then there's all the illness stuff, I probably can't have kids anyway, because of my blocked tubes, chlamydia, the clap, and then if I do manage to conceive, I'm a million times more likely to miscarry than most people, because of all my illnesses, my weird cervix, etc. That's if it's not an ectopic pregnancy which I'm even *more* prone to . . . Every time I get a symptom, I think, chlamydia. Not that again, not the ugly spectre of infertility, that old ghost, come to haunt me again. Again.

Thursday: *On the phone.*

B : It's so difficult —

J : — being a Woman . . .

B : No — wow, you're there already? I'm still at the transvestite stage —

J : Join the queue!

B : No, really, I used to feel just like a transvestite, I used to wear these trousers, very very tapered *indeed*, and you know, a sweater, and I had these high heels, the heels were worn down a bit, I really liked them but the heels were a little too high for me — and then I had this really lovely handbag of my godmother's, with a little handle, and I'd wear it as a shoulder bag, you know, tucked right *under*, but it would slide down, of course, and I'd end up holding it by the handle, in my hand —and I remember at work one time, I was working in the Merchandise Mart in Chicago, I remember this woman who worked there looked at me one day and said, "I see, when you were a little girl someone told you that grown-up ladies wear high heels and carry little *hand* bags." There I was, tottering slightly in these shoes, and clutching this bag — like a child, or a transvestite.

J : That's it — dressing up in mummy's clothes. That's all we can do.

B : Yes, but let's face it, we're fondly imagining that there's some femininity out there somewhere that *isn't* like that, that's real, authentic. The madonna, the woman with the child in her arms. And lots of people kneeling at her feet, preferably.

J : It must be awful to have a baby and feel just as strange about it as we feel in our high heels and handbags. I expect it happens all the time.

B : What a ghastly thought.

Monday: *On the phone.*

J : We went to see these people, these old friends of Stephen's, and you know, they live in this fantastic house, and she's really *stunning*, she's got Kirghiz eyes, and he's great, they're both great, and they have this sweet kid, in pyjamas, going to bed, and I just thought, I'll never have that, never never never, I'll never have a house with high ceilings and long windows and a garden with a *tree* in it, and it was like I was just overcome with envy — the sense of loss — like it's *too late*.

B : But why is it too late?

J : It's just that you make choices, and all along the way you have to recognize what you're giving up, what's falling by the wayside. It's like you realize what you're precluding by being the person you are.

B : This sounds ridiculous to me.

J : My friend Penelope's analyst always used to say: Envy, use it! You want it, get it! Don't writhe in torment, do it! I always thought this was the most useful thing anybody's analyst had ever said *ever*.

B : So?

J : So I don't *really* want to live that Other Life, I just feel this loss, when I know I can't, when I'm forced to acknowledge that it's not an option.

B : It's like in AA they say, this is not a dress rehearsal.

J : Mmm.

Tuesday: *On the phone.*

J : Can I read you this bit I found about narcissism and having babies?

B : If you must.

J : It kills me, this stuff. He says: *Even for narcissistic women, whose attitude to men remains cool,* check it out, *there is a road to complete object love.* That's what we want, right? Object Love. So, he says: *In the child which they bear, a part of their own body confronts them like an extraneous object, to which, starting out from their narcissism, they can then give complete object love.* I love that bit about the extraneous object, it's like a horror movie.

B : I think it's all nonsense. I mean when it comes to real life.

J : I think it's true.

B : Not in practice, not really.

J : Really.

B : Jesus. No wonder you're so fucked up.

J : Thanks a lot. I had another dream.

B : OK. Fire away.

J : I don't think there's much interpreting to do, it fits right in with your theory about my work . . .

B : Tell me the dream, I've got to go.

J : In the dream I was going to *adopt* a newborn baby, because I wanted one *right away.* But when it appeared, it was a fucked-up little girl (*already* damaged, a girl with a history), instead of the baby *boy* (now it was gender specific, suddenly) that I'd expected. I sent her back, or thought of sending her back.

B : And how is it about your work?

J : Well I think it's about my wish that one day I'll just wake up and suddenly *become* this different person, you know, I imagine this entirely *new* (phallic?) writing will be mine —but of course it can't happen, I'll always only have the confused, confusing —

B : Castrated —

J : — fucked-up little girl. It's what I've *got.*

B : That sounds logical. So once again it's not about babies at all.

J : Nope, that's right. Just about me. I thought, if I ever had a daughter, I could name her Chlamydia.

Friday: *On the phone.*

B : I had this dream, in this dream I was a woman, and — I mean, I was *specifically* a woman, which is *most* unusual — anyway, I was this woman, but . . .

Tuesday: *On the phone.*

B : I had this friend who could never imagine herself envied. It was as if she had a block, she couldn't even contemplate it for a second. I figured it was all about insisting that she was the most deprived of all, and for me to suggest that she did have something, anything, that others could envy, was like being very cruel to her, saying something horrible, because she needed so much to be the envier, and never the envied.

J : People like that get really carried away when the wheel turns, though, and they really enjoy being in a position of the envied one. Like all those years of suppressed showing off, of denying you have anything at all — when things change, and they can finally afford to admit it, it's amazing, they're the ones who really dig it. Narcissistic gratification. They positively gloat.

B : I don't know if that's true. I don't think so. I think most of the time they never get there, they remain enviers forever.

Suddenly Jeanie saw herself from outside: enviable. It was like looking over her own shoulder, like when the camera is just behind the protagonist, placing him firmly in the picture. Most of the time she felt detached from the world, which, like a movie, swirled on without her. But suddenly she saw herself, in enviable terms. No kids encumbering, no tiny hands clutching at her knees, no baby vomit on her black sweater. Independence: her own flat, with windows, and pictures on the wall. The noisy street outside, buses rumble past, to remind her of this busy city: no gentle tree-lined streets for her. No pram-pushing down the tree-lined street, the baby carry-cot on the back seat of the Renault, off to the giant Sainsbury's, stocking up. A freezer. None of that. She went out, with Stephen, almost every night. Occasionally, cheques came in the post, for work she'd done. Books arrived, to review. People telephoned, asking her to appear here, or there. She kept trying different hairdressers. She bought shoes. Sometimes she received unsolicited gifts, in the form of notes from people who admired her work. Somehow, most of the time she forgot about these things. They were invisible to her. She longed for a child.

Jeanie went to visit a friend with kids. It was hell. She saw herself from outside, suddenly: enviable.

My longing for a child percolates through the semi-permeable stone of these dark grey days, poisoning the well. Conversations are riddled with obscure or secret references to this possibility, as if my ears are always pricked, hoping for the signal that will quell my anxiety, make the decision. If only I could give it up, or pursue it; as it is, I'm frozen, my feet set in cement, stuck in this moment of the mourning of possibility.

Tears in the bath, hot, lying in hot water with hot tears on my face, my hand flat on my belly, suddenly remembering feeling so sick this morning, and thinking: *maybe I'm pregnant.* An immediate sensation of terror, then some rapid calculations, ovulation, sex, nine months from now would be? Horror. Then, with no warning, tears, for my longing, to have a baby inside me, is complete and overwhelming.

Note: Melanie Klein's (staggering) contention that little girls don't find the same satisfaction in masturbation that little boys do, because of their sense of internal organs, the "receptive quality" of the vagina which produces a longing for penetration. Of course, I didn't know I had a vagina, so my receptive quality must be impaired. But there's a difference between a wish to be penetrated (which is all about crossing a boundary, the thin line that holds my body together, the surface of my skin), and a wish to have something inside you (which could be a baby, or a penis, or an ideal image of oneself, even?). Possibly. I used to imagine myself like a small figurine inside the great shell of my body. As if my body were hollow, and there were great dark voids between the surface of my skin and the little person inside me. That's very different to imagining a baby, who is always curled up perfectly or under water. These hot tears, now, salty like the amniotic fluid in the womb.

Tracing ambivalence, how does it go: first, the shocking thought. Nausea. Terror. Calculations: when did I ovulate, when did we fuck, when is my period due, when would the baby be born? Horrified disbelief: it's not possible. Pregnancy test: you can buy kits at the chemist. You can go to your GP. Sudden thought of abnormality: my blocked tubes (ectopic), my diseases (spontaneous abortion), my fucked-up cervix. My inability to give birth. More terror. And then the thought of the little child inside me, possibly, and tears, too many tears, in the hot water. Feeling sick.

A book would perform all the functions of a baby, she thought, writing another book. It would occupy her time and energy, make demands, be messy and shitty and wet and uncontrollable, and it would scream at times, and at times it would sleep (she would sleep), and in the end, just like a baby, it would speak to her, saying things she didn't expect. On the borders of sleep, hypnagogic, she pictured a baby, wrapped in white lacy robes, wearing a little bonnet, and then, like Alice holding the pig, she saw herself holding, like a baby in her arms, a large round log of wood, with sawed ends, coarse bark, in a lacy bonnet and white baby blanket. She knew it represented the raw material of the paper of the book that would take the place of her wish for a baby. It was heavy and solid, as writing isn't, heavy and solid as her wish. She woke up, and decided to *transfer* her desire. Later Bette pointed out that log means a kind of book, a journal. Jeanie felt that sense of flurried excitement, the elation that comes when one inadvertently comes upon the dreamwork.

When I had PID, it was amazing, how painful it was. I remember that I couldn't stop moving. I kept writhing, I had to keep moving, turning, on my bed. At one point Stephen touched me, gently, he put his hand on my side, and I couldn't bear it, I recoiled. Rose was here from New York, and Connie, and Stephen — all these horrified faces, looking down at me, they were pale with horror. And me just writhing in pain.

It was really awful, but there's some comic bits . . . Stephen amazingly had just sprained his ankle. I'd made him jump over a tree in Kew Gardens, he'd jumped over my bed suddenly and I was incredibly impressed, I never knew he could *jump*, and then a few days later, when we were at Kew with the Russians, I said, for a joke, Stephen can jump! And so he did, and sprained his ankle, badly, and was in the most amazing pain. He drank a lot of rum, and smoked dope, and refused to go to hospital. And, like, the *next day*, I suddenly collapsed. I was alone in the house, and

Rose was arriving from New York, and I began to be in the most terrible pain.

I went out, to throw myself into the doctor's surgery across the road, but they were closed between 12 and 2.30, and I was standing in the street in the most terrible pain, it was five past twelve, and I thought I saw one of the doctors from the practice a little way down the street, but I was too embarrassed to accost him, to say, are you a doctor, help me. This is a sign of how my brain wasn't functioning any more. I was completely desperate. I left the keys for Rose at the off-licence across the road, and collapsed into bed. The telephone rang, it was Rebecca Marshall to ask me to lunch, and I was all right for a bit and then I was crying uncontrollably, I couldn't breathe or speak, and she realized I was alone and completely freaking out and said, I'll be right over. So Rose walked in from the airport, full of beans, and then Rebecca appeared, with a flower, and I was (literally) writhing in agony. It seemed impossible to wait two hours until the surgery reopened. I had no idea what to do. Rose said, don't you know any other doctors? This was a revelation. I remembered my mother's private doctor. I telephoned, they said it was OK to come and see his colleague. It was in Wimpole Street though and I had no idea how I was going to get there. I said, I'm not sure I'm going to be able to drive. Rose said: We'll take a taxi. I had completely forgotten that taxis existed.

At that time I had this IUD, I'd had it for about nine months, it was an experimental IUD called the T-Nova, it could be left in for four years, and it had copper *and* silver wrapped around it. I pictured it like an ear-ring embedded in my womb. The FPA had refused to give me an IUD, they said if I ever wanted to have children I shouldn't, not with my history. That the risk of infection was too strong. Then I fell in love with Stephen, and we would do sex all the time, and I was extremely anxious about getting pregnant, mainly the problem of renewing spermicide, because even then I couldn't use those pessaries, anyway I was terribly worried about it and I decided to get an IUD so I wouldn't have to worry. I tricked the FPA into giving it to me, I said that I'd already had the appointment they insist on, to discuss the IUD, the pros and cons, I lied, basically, to get them to give me the IUD right away. And they did, and they gave me a new, experimental one, with silver as well as copper, which I pictured as a beneficent ear-ring nestled in my womb. Until I started writhing with pain.

Pelvic Inflammatory Disease is caused by bacteria getting inside your uterus and travelling up your fallopian tubes. They think they climb up the nylon string that's attached to the IUD, the string they use to pull it out. Chlamydia is the name of a particularly lethal one of these string-climbing organisms. It's only recently been isolated, and named, so it isn't in the books yet, the only people who've heard of it are the women who've had it. Anyway, when you have an orgasm, your uterus makes a spasmodic movement, that can actually suck things into itself, so the IUD is really most suitable for non-orgasmic women who've already had children. Because then infertility isn't such a problem.

The Wimpole Street doctor said, it's either a pelvic infection or it's appendicitis. I'd been unable to sit still in the taxi, continuous writhing, but the pain left me almost completely when I was flat on my back on the examination table in his enormous office. This often happens to me with doctors; I am so frightened of them my symptoms disappear. He gave me a scrip for a double dose of antibiotics. He described how the pain would change if it was appendicitis, and how in that case, I should go to the hospital. He said he didn't believe that IUDs cause pelvic infection and there was no need to take it out, although some doctors did remove it when this happened. I went home and went to bed. It was Friday. I spent the weekend in bed, too ill to eat, even.

I took every painkiller in the house — Italian diarrhoea pills with opium, some leftover Distalgesic. The pain was completely hypnotic, I was unable to think about anything else. Then on Monday morning things were suddenly much worse. Connie called in the doctor from the surgery across the street, an emergency, she said, and he came right away. I was way out there, far beyond any ability to make decisions or even speak. The doctor was furious he hadn't been called sooner. He said he would take the IUD out at three that afternoon. After he left I fell into a state of abject terror; the terror even overcame the pain. I remembered all the times an IUD had been put in or taken out, I remembered the time I screamed as they pulled out the Copper 7, the first one, at the health clinic at college, in 1975. I couldn't face it. I was in a state of abject terror, I couldn't cry or talk, it was just this terrible gasping, and writhing. And then my body saved me. It was as if I just couldn't take any more, I'd reached the limit. I sank into a heavy sleep, in that white room, I became unconscious. There was no warning: the pain receded, sleep appeared out of nowhere, I knew nothing.

At ten to three, Connie woke me up, time to go to the doctor. I was so sleepy it was like having taken a load of tranquillizers. Instead of the writhing, sobbing, out of control, flailing terror, I had become a heavy, pale body, almost sleep-walking across the street. I asked the doctor for intravenous valium; he said, we'll try to do it without, but I promise if you can't bear it, we'll give you something. This seemed reasonable; I was capable of being reasonable. It was as if I was in slow motion; having been in a panic, high pitched, shrieking, I was sleep-walking, very very calm.

On the table, lying on my back, Connie held my hand and talked to me. The doctor put the speculum in, and couldn't find my cervix. He dug around with it for a while. He was somewhat in awe of our tremendous presence, rather wonderfully and appropriately humble, so when I calmly said, I suggest you take the speculum out, and stick your finger in to *feel* where the cervix is, and *then* put the speculum back in, he wasn't offended, incredibly, and he did it.

The first time an IUD was put into me, a nurse came in, to literally hold my hand and talk about *anything* else — what I was studying, where I was born, etc. This is incredibly irritating, but very effective as a distraction. It's almost impossible to reply politely to a stranger's questions, and at the same time hold your whole body in fear, anticipating the moment of pain. Unthinking, Connie and I automatically did this. I said, this is so funny, it reminds me of the story when I was born. Connie said, yes. I said, you know it. And *she* said (brilliantly), tell Dr Green. So I launched into this primal anecdote, occupying the upper part (so to speak) of my mind, while my body took deep breaths, laid out flat with my legs spread wide, readying itself for this moment of intense pain. I was expecting, or it was expecting this pain to be inconceivable, but there was also some sense that when the IUD was out, it would be the beginning of the end of this, the beginning of the possibility of getting better. At the same time (this was part of the terror before my sleep) I knew Dr Green wasn't an expert; he wasn't a doctor who took out IUDs every day, like at the FPA. In the terror, I'd reasoned with myself, before the sleep came, I'd said, what is the worst that can happen? The worst is that my uterus will be perforated when the IUD is taken out and I will never be able to have children. This is *not* the worst thing in the whole world. It's terrible, but *much* worse things can happen to you. It's as if I made my peace, so to say, with this worst, persuaded myself it wasn't unbearable, and then I could crash out.

On the table, of course, I didn't think of that; I thought of nothing, something else entirely. As the doctor tinkered around in my vagina, I told the story of my mother, how she insisted that the baby was coming, no one believed her, she insisted on going to the hospital, and then she was left alone in a labour room with a student nurse, and eventually, suddenly, this *foot* appeared (my foot), coming out of her vagina, whereupon the nurse exclaimed, Jesus Christ! and ran out of the room. That's the end of the story. After years of hearing it, I finally asked her, so what did you do then? And she said, I took hold of that foot and pulled as hard as I can, I wanted you *out* of there.

And Connie was laughing, and the doctor pulled, and I felt this slight sensation, of something slipping deep inside me, and Dr Green said, it's out, it's all over, and I gasped, I said, I don't believe it, it's out? And the doctor said, it was half out already, it was digging into your cervix, that's why you were in such terrible pain.

I don't remember what happened after that. The relief blew through me like cool air, filling me up, no more pain, no more terror. There was an image of a T-shaped ear-ring with its caul of blood and phlegm, I was so glad to have this thing *out* of me. I hadn't realized how impossible it was for me to imagine getting well, being well, I couldn't *picture* my uterus without this silver and copper object, this T-Nova in there, poisoning me.

I stayed in bed for weeks, I was amazingly ill, and slowly I got better again. I watched Notorious on TV. And it was almost funny to remember that mental argument, when I persuaded myself that infertility wasn't the worst thing that can happen to you, because of course what really would have been unthinkable, what would have been impossible to bear, was if the pain I was feeling then were to go on. And in a way, coming up with the idea of a life unable to have children was, like the story of my birth, coming up with a distraction, in the form of a rationalization, in order to get away from the agony of my body, and my terror of more pain to come.

The analyst was bored.

People suffered so much, it was unbelievably wearing to maintain his defences, keep the psychic raincoat on as they poured their unhappy words over him, sitting silently there. (He wouldn't call it a psychic raincoat. That was wrong.)

People suffered so much, more of the same, more of the same.

Sometimes his interest would be piqued by a new combination, almost like the pleasant surprise of seeing someone wearing intentionally clashing colours, an emerald green hat angled on shocking pink hair, different colour fluorescent socks. (He doesn't think like that, this is all wrong.)

People suffered so much, it was hard to keep up the façade, hard not to suffer with them. Sometimes that simple process, of maintaining his defences, took up almost all his energy. (He doesn't use words like energy.)

The analyst was bored.

On and on, this endless suffering, and not one of his patients had made a joke for days. It goes without saying that he wasn't allowed to; occasionally he didn't even allow himself to laugh at one of theirs, replying instead with one of the classic formulae, so sententious, about how it really isn't very funny is it, etc. etc. Turning bitter laughter into tears, that was part of his job. And never crying himself, refusing laughter often, to get at the deeper feelings that he knew were there. November and February were the worst months for jokes; he blamed the weather. As Christmas and Easter, with their long breaks, approached, the misery and resentment of the patients, soon to be deprived of the analyst, often generated sequences of black comedy unmatched in any sphere. It was always the most intelligent clients who had to be deflected from these forays into bitter humour. But most of the time, it was familiar territory, mothers and fathers and lovers and how hurt, how damaged and hurt we all are.

What does the analyst envy? I envy the analyst; what does the analyst envy?

To Jeanie the question seemed extraordinarily profound. It was like turning the tables, upsetting the couch. As a rule, they were meant to be concerned only with Jeanie's feelings, her very private agonies and pleasures. Of course, imagining the analyst's envy was only another way of putting Jeanie's unconscious fantasies into words, bringing them to mind. That's what the analyst would have thought. But for Jeanie, alone in her room, it was a revelation to even consider the analyst, the great man, as possibly envious. For her, it felt like a huge leap into objectivity, into a sense of real history. It also seemed like an unanswerable question.

The analyst envies other analysts. The analyst envies younger analysts starting out on their training analysis, when the whole world of psychoanalysis is just opening up and still has its tremendous depth and glamour. The analyst envies those patients who terminate, who are not seduced into the endless project of becoming an analyst themselves. (There are three ways to terminate: the analyst leaves the country, the patient leaves the country, the patient decides to become an analyst. It wasn't a joke.) The analyst envies those patients who leave the country? She stopped. That didn't sound right, especially as she was intending to leave the country. The analyst envies the artist, who has access to the unconscious in ways the analyst cannot understand or control. Speaking as an artist, she felt the analyst ought to envy this. Perhaps he didn't though, perhaps that was part of the problem. She felt that she bought his line on what she ought to envy, the house, the garden, the kids, the family, the career, it was pretty easy to be persuaded that all one's feelings of exclusion and distress were valid, substantial, and that you really should devote yourself to getting some of these things. But maybe he didn't see what she had, something that maybe he ought to want more, to envy.

Monday: *On the couch.*

J: The problem is, babies, yes babies, I want one. Badly.

Dr Q: Yes.

J: But if I want one, if I allow myself to want one — it's a problem, because it opens up a whole new can of gynaecological worms, so to speak.

Dr Q: ...

J: I mean, it's difficult to choose to want something that *maybe* I won't be able to have — because of all the predispositions and illnesses and things.

Dr Q: Go on.

J: You see it would be a bit of a *risk* really, I don't want to go through a series of miscarriages or whatever, and maybe not be able to have one; it's a real risk — of possibly plunging yet further into the nightmare black abyss of illness and doctors and gynaecological trouble, just a reconfirmation of the sense of damage, my sense of femininity as damage, damagedness.

Dr Q: ...

J: On the other hand, I think possibly I would be someone who would be very happy if I *did* have a baby, because it would be a *making good* of all this nightmare sense of damage and illness and difficulty that's so established, integral, like tiny roots through my body. I think I would be very *pleased* if out of all this dark abyss of gynaecology and trouble would come this good thing, this baby.

Dr Q: Yes.

J: So once again all this stuff just comes back to fantasies about *oneself.* I always used to be so vehement about the rights of the child — you know, really angry at the idea of parents reproducing for their own egotistical reasons, and yet here I am, finding this business of thinking of having a baby in order to make good my own bodily history *makes sense.* It's weird.

Dr Q: ...

J: I suspect it's my age, you know, when you're fourteen you think it's outrageous that your parents had you without really *meaning* to, that is, for their own foolish reasons. I always figured they were like, on automatic, anyway, the fifties family and its two point four kids. And now I'm approaching the reproductive deadline, of *course* having babies is something you do for your own pleasure — what other reason could there be?

Dr Q: What other reason do you think there could be?

The analyst envies people who don't do jobs like this.

Analysis as a profession was like being a dentist: there were those who advocated flossing, those who did extractions, those who concentrated on straightening teeth and those who were mostly concerned with preventing disease. But basically it was the same, probing into the wet dark rotten inner recesses of someone's head, overcoming inevitable disgust at signs of neglect and corruption, the furry tongue, the blackened molar, the broken, jagged edge of a damaged tooth, all this in the higher cause of scientific detachment, medical objectivity, the only sure path to enlightenment. Using the same shiny instruments over and over, those sententious phrases he absolutely relied on, with the same problems emerging again and again. The sexual element was there too. Lying down is always a difficult pleasure, and everyone has sadomasochistic dentist fantasies, everyone knows that sensation of being at his mercy, the frisson of terror that lies within one's necessary submission and dependence. And of course dentistry, like psychoanalysis, was fundamentally all about pain, pain and beauty.

Jeanie found it hard to imagine that anyone would ever want to be a dentist.

INTERLUDE

Corinne sat in the huge room, as pale light flooded through the tall windows, throwing bright oblongs over the long tables. The enormous rooms were almost completely deserted, and the air had the warm soft hush of old libraries. Corinne was perfectly happy, a scattering of open and closed books and papers making a semi-circle around her place, as she turned the pages of the big dictionary, pen in hand, making notes.

She wrote:

Notes on the Pre-Oedipal Phase
1. Bi-polar mood swings: rhapsody and rage (R & R). Acute pleasure of both states.
2. Real frustration leads to state of rage; real satisfaction to rhapsody. Too simplistic?
3. Constant sensational flux, infinite gradations of sensation, detailed specificity of the surface and interior of the body.
4. Boundaries, thresholds, the liminal sensations. Oral, anal, genital: the gateways between inside and outside.
5. Food and excrement prove the liminal, constitute the boundaries. Take food in, shit and piss it out. Using these membranous gateways makes sense of inside and outside.
6. Endless hallucinogenic psychic experience. Impossible to divorce fr. bodily experience. Hypnagogic states.
7. Things outside: source of R & R. Assoc. of colours, sounds, smells, etc. with presence/absence of M.
8. Rage: classic wish to scratch, gouge, bite, scrape, burst, break, obliterate the body of M.
9. Rhapsody: no division, oceanic, therefore no conflict (??) — *or* the sense of omnipotence: either all-powerful or completely frustrated. Things can't get better or worse, they're either perfect or intolerable.
10. No boredom. (Unlike some places . . .)

Outside the celestial psychoanalytic library, Corinne was bored. You were allowed to do whatever you liked, here, even leave. In a sense you were ignored. Occasionally Corinne suspected her research project was motivated by envy and revenge. Never having been a mother herself, she'd invented the perfect form of attack. One was supposed to have left all that behind, needless to say, but Corinne didn't want to, she held on to the thrilling intensity of the unconscious like holding on to the bar of a roller-coaster, returning again to that ecstatic, shrieking subjection.

She couldn't wait.

THE SUDDEN DEATHS OF CHILDREN

Jeanie had this theory, that having children changes the terms of your relationship with death, it brings you closer to your own mortality. This is partly because of the immortality a child (possibly) promises, the sheer immortality of genes, and then there's the possibility of starting over: the kid'll do it differently, the same, that is, but better. The child both fends off death, and outlives you; it replaces you, in some sense. And partly she thought it brings you closer to death simply because the child might die. When thinking about the possibility of having a baby, Jeanie thought about the baby's death a lot.

Eventually she raised this problem with her sister, Louise, whose son was seventeen now. She said, "No, I never imagined that Paul could die, I never thought of Paul *dying*." Jeanie said, "You're the most repressed person I've ever met, or maybe the most optimistic, the most well-adjusted." Louise said, "Thinking about death when you think about having a baby seems a little weird to me." Jeanie said, "It's logical, it's not just me being anxious — kids die *all the time*. All the time. Kids get run over *all the time*." "No," Louise said, "no, kids don't get run over all the time."

It was hard for Jeanie to decide who was right. She knew that kids *did* get run over, every day, and she knew too that she herself was very fearful of attachment, because any attachment always carries within it a darker implication, the risk of loss. And she envied her sister, her sister's son, with a stony, poisonous envy that burst out in the dark cry of why her not me? Even so, being terrified of possible loss, of being abandoned or bereaved, always seemed extremely logical to Jeanie. It wasn't mad. It was reasonable. She continued to anticipate the sudden deaths of children.

Jeanie made a list.

> 1. There was a girl at college, she was an oddball, no one liked her much; she had a sort of shadowy, slimy aspect, and she looked scared, which, since 'most everyone was in a permanent state of terror, was the one thing that was completely socially unacceptable. A story was told about this girl, that she'd killed a sibling when she was a child, she'd killed her baby brother. She was about five or six, and she'd taken the baby out of his cot or basket or baby chair, and walked onto the balcony and dropped him over the railing. We were terribly impressed. Her loneliness suddenly seemed sinister. Of course we didn't fully believe the story, but you always remembered it when you saw her cringing around the corridors.
> 2. I remember a little girl who tried to put the new baby in a wastepaper basket, to get rid of it. Anita's three-year-old boy was overheard by his grandmother singing little songs to himself about the new baby and riding on a train and a terrible crash where everybody dies.
> 3. Oliver and his partner had this baby, and Oliver's older brother and his wife, who's Italian, drove down to the

country to see the new baby, five weeks old, and they had lunch, and the new mother put the baby in her pram outside, by the kitchen door, for her nap, and the Italian sister-in-law (who had a couple of kids of her own) said, it's so cold, you English, you're so tough on the little thing, but the new mother said it was fine, and at the end of the nap suddenly the baby was completely dead, an unexplained cot death. And the mother tried to resuscitate the baby, sitting on the stairs, and then she carried her through the house, so everyone could say goodbye to the baby, and then it was over.

4. Anna's sister had a baby, a boy, and he was crying one morning and they left him, he was six months old, and then he was quiet, and then she went in and he was dead. She said she knew immediately that he was dead.

5. My cousin had a baby who pulled a chest of drawers over on herself when she was about two and a half. It killed her.

6. Sometimes babies die when they're born too early, when they're premature. That happened to Rebecca's baby.

7. Mahler wrote songs about his kids dying. I don't remember what they're called.

8. Kids get run over all the time.

On the bed: *Jeanie and Stephen were lying on the bed, talking.*

J : Do you remember that painting, it was a picture of a sky just *full* of naked babies? Spanish, seventeenth-century, eighteenth-century?

S : Yes, I think so, it was a painting of purgatory?

J : Mmm, limbo. These were all the unbaptized infants, all the untold millions of babies who die. Perinatal mortality rates in seventeenth-century Spain and the practice of baptism . . .

But it must include miscarriages, and abortions — although maybe aborted babies are deemed to be little martyrs, victims —

S : — more sinned against than sinning —

J : So they get to go to heaven.

S : But in this scheme of things heaven and purgatory are very close, right? I mean, limbo — is almost as pleasant as heaven?

J : I just wonder whether the evolution of cherubs, the whole business of covering a church or a painting with millions of naked bodies of babies, is necessarily related to the infant mortality rate.

S : There *is* a difference between heaven and limbo . . .

J : Who is it that goes on about how children's bodies are the real source of pleasure for people, not sex —

S : I always thought that was crazy. I also think it's wrong — children are continually being touched by people, and it always annoys me.

J : Why?

S : It's like, after a certain stage of self-consciousness, the child can't initiate physical contact with adults (except its parents, or immediate family), but they constantly have to submit to total strangers ruffling their hair or making them smile or giving them sweets. It's like, just sitting on the bus, children are at the mercy of everyone else's desire.

J : We'd all like to be the child — the child is so beautiful, so *lovely.*

S : No, everyone wants to be the one the child loves — the one the child runs to, or responds to. We all want to have the rights of a mother, we want to take liberties.

J : It's because the child is so *sweet.*

S : Maybe *you* want to be the child, admired by everybody —

J : Yes, it must be awful, being jealous of a kid. I'm just struck, though, what a weird thing to paint. What kind of pleasure is derived from a painting of hundreds of dead babies?

S : But they're not dead, they're pink and rosy and healthy, flying around, happy as clams.

J : Surely they must remind you of your dead babies? I mean, your seventeenth-century dead babies?

S : Yes, and here they are, alive and well and living in limbo. Having a fine old time.

J : Mmm. Do you remember that church in Mexico? The one covered in babies?

S : With the babies carved in plaster.

J : That's right. It's the same sort of thing, really. Incredible *excess*, this multiplicity of interchangeable baby bodies, identically round and sweet and pink. Undifferentiated. Millions of them, millions of dead babies.

S : Jeanie, I know you insist on thinking of them as dead, but surely the whole point is that they're *not*. It's a representation of dead babies as now not-dead.

J : Same difference, almost.

S : Anyway, they're angels, aren't they? Little cherubs?

J : What *is* a cherub?

S : It's a baby with wings.

J : Like a bat's a mouse with wings.

S : A rat with wings.

J : Stop!

Remembering what it was like living in a family, hell on wheels, realizing I've done everything I can to make sure this, my own house, is as different as possible, to refuse the nightmarish misunderstanding, the mistaken closeness, taking of liberties, the endless exchange of identification and projection, elaborate dance of misrecognition, the cruelty based on the false authority of adult over child, the complete lack of physical privacy, the absence of polite detachment . . . One day I came home from school and found my absolutely favourite thirties crêpe dress in a plastic washing-up bowl full of bleach. It was ruined. My mother said she had mistaken it for a rag. This I found impossible to believe. Melanie Klein says girls are terrified their mothers will destroy a) their beauty, and b) their capacity to have a baby. So why? Why, when family life is so loathsome? The intensity of biology, impelled to genetic immortality, narcissism, the logic of desire, moving on and on, always utterly wanting, always insatiable, as one thing after another disappears, un-marked, into the vast blackness of its gigantic gob . . .

An overwhelming sense of loss, when I think of how I don't see my friends, my girl friends who are married now, having babies, the women with kids. I can't bear to see them. Is this sense of loss a cover for my envy? Mourning *as always* so much easier than my conflicted feelings. I (must have) wanted to do away with the baby, to get rid of it, when it was my mother's baby, my sister's baby. I'm frightened of that — of taking the mother's place? It seems, undeniably, not for me, and at the same time, infinitely desirable. I joke with Stephen about domesticity, my persistent thoughts of the scratch on the new linoleum, my latest obsession, I say, I haven't got a baby, but I have got a *scratch*. The real woman, domesticated at last. I begin to see the absurdity of my position, and stop (for a moment) insisting that I've lost everything I could possibly want.

The child sets the seal on the narcissistic love affair. We love each other, in misrecognition, seeing you as a lovely version of myself. But the baby we produce really is a lovely version of me *and* you. It's perfect. We can adore it, even though you're jealous.

Today Stephen and I found ourselves talking about "the baby". "I'd be jealous," Stephen said, "— you'd spend all your love on *the baby*." "But you'd love *the baby* too," I said. He said, "Yes, of course —the little *brat*." He said it could be called Potlatch, or Robot. I said Potlatch was OK as a middle name, perhaps. Diplomatically.

I picture us, in madonna and child mode, Stephen somehow draped at knee level, admiration of the child, or adoration, I guess, of the child on my lap.

If you allow yourself to want, something, something opens up in you, the abyss; you sense the great icy wastes of lack, a wide black sky over polar wastes, vast and desolate. You become once again the deprived child, the insecure, underprivileged, left out, lost girl and her enormous, gaping heart.

When I get a little of what I want, when I'm given a touch, a glimpse, the barest edge of love or recognition, it's like icebergs breaking up, the abyss of wanting yawns inside me, huge alligator jaws spread wide and I'm at the mercy of a yearning so vast it's impossible. I want everything.

Boa constrictors first squeeze their prey to death, surrounding their victim with coils of emotion, and then swallow it whole. This is possible because the jaw unhooks and can spread very wide. That's what I feel like: the boa constrictor about to swallow a huge animal which my violent emotion has just squeezed to death.

On the plane: *Jeanie was scared of flying. Stephen wasn't.*

J : I *hate* taking all these drugs, metronidazole, doxycycline, I hate all this chlamydia shit. I had a dream this morning, I was kneeling, crying, bare knees on cold floor, before a priest, and he says, knowing I've come to take communion (which I've never done, in real life) he says very aggressive, "So you have come to shoot up? It's all right," he says, "I shoot God too. I visit the shooting gallery. Is that what you've come for?" I didn't know the ritual phrase that you're meant to say, father forgive me for I have sinned, I didn't know, I was crying, and he absolved me, he placed the host in my mouth — but the dream ended before I could taste it, because I've never tasted it, I guess. I woke up.

S : Sounds like a visit to the doctor.

J : Yes, but it's about babies too, about all this infertility stuff.

S : How?

J : When I was fourteen I refused to get confirmed, and my mother was furious and she said, "Just don't ever take communion when your baby dies, when something awful happens and you need comfort!" Which of course I was very struck by, I couldn't imagine wanting to take communion in that circumstance, it seemed very foreign to me. I mean, I couldn't imagine having a baby at all, and then the idea of the baby dying seemed even more remote . . .

S : So all this fear of babies dying is fear of the malevolent, eviscerating mother, no?

J : You mean *my* mother?

S : Who wishes dead babies on you —

J : But I *chose* not to have kids, remember, and it's like Connie's mother always said, be very careful what you wish for, because you *always* get it.

S : Your wish becomes your punishment.

J : It's like a figure eight. [*Jeanie drew a figure eight with her finger on the back of the seat in front of her.*] Whatever mourning I have to do, the mourning I'm doing now for babies I maybe won't have in the future, it's like it has to *double back*, and draw in the old mourning, the old wish, that's past any possibility of restoration or salvage . . .

S : I think if you want to have a baby, we should have one.

J : I know, darling. I know.

When Jeanie was a small child, her family lived in Italy, and for her sister's eighth birthday, her parents took her to Egypt, and Jeanie was left behind. There's something fundamental about these things, about such early losses — not only *not* seeing Egypt, not only lack, but your sister so emphatically having something you don't. Nothing can ever compensate for those visions of the pyramids that she didn't see. And possibly, since her relation to Egypt existed solely on the level of fantasy, as *envy*, there's something irreducible, something very important about it. It was hers in a different way, her own to play with — to give herself (my Egypt) and to throw away (I was never taken there, I was left behind, too little). The child always envies a fantasy of something else, the child only envies what she doesn't know.

The snapshots showed her father and Louise on two camels, and her mother on a dark horse, with robed men standing on the sand, pyramids in the background. It was 1960. She was surprised that her mother was too scared to ride a camel.

Jeanie stared at these photos with a kind of wondering disbelief: how is it possible that she, and not I, should have seen these things? These things were, inevitably, the Pyramids, the Sphinx, the Nile. Mummies. The camels, which they rode. It was like a story, unbelievable. There were camels in her ark. To ride a camel in the desert: inconceivable. The photos proved it true. That made it worse.

Her sister, Louise, upon her return, would mash together a little lump of butter and honey, to spread on her toast at breakfast. She'd learned to do this in Egypt, where they ate croissants, on a balcony, in the sun. When Jeanie tried to imitate this, to mash butter and honey, Louise was vehement, you can't do it, that's not the right way. They brought back a picture of the head of Nefertiti. Jeanie used to study the neck with pleasure.

When Jeanie grew up, she fell in love with Stephen, and he took her to Egypt.

Egypt's all about death, Jeanie thought, the frozen immobility of death, in the dry sand, dry air of the desert. Death and permanence.

The Nile valley was wet and green, and then there was a sudden line between the desert and fertility, a line where the lush green just stopped, and beyond there was only endless sand. Nothing between here and Libya, the guide said, when they visited the pyramids.

She conceived their child at the Old Cataract Hotel in Aswan, one clear morning. She enjoyed being pregnant, the companionship of this interior visitor. While the child seemed fictional at times, her body reminded her of its constant presence.

The evil eye is a look of envy; we ward it off with the image of an eye, returning the look. In Egypt, the eye is in the middle of a hand, as if the upraised hand warded off, and the look, reflected in the image of the eye, returned to the envious.

The hotel in Luxor was on an island in the Nile; there was a swimming pool, and an Arab orchestra, and a sunset arena. Jeanie sat and watched the sun set, the slow river turning gold and silver, bright green leaves merging into black, the clear sky and wide open desert in the distance. Strange birds sang. Jeanie was terribly happy.

CODA

I was perched in the little Temple of Minerva up behind the eucalyptus grove, looking down over the river and contemplating the view. I'm very fond of that temple, its delicate columns of golden stone, and the lovely bench beneath the statue. I was sitting there, thinking about the invention of the ha-ha, a grassy ditch designed to blur the division between garden and farm, a sunken fence, so that the visual transition from lawn to field is gently effected, almost imperceptible. I watched the sunlight reflecting off the silvery eucalyptus leaves below, as they shuddered slightly in the puffing wind. The transition, from inside to outside, that the ha-ha visually dissolves, is less symbolically pressing here, where Nature is never inclement or malign. Still, you don't want the sheep to eat the peonies, do you?

Corinne appeared, stepping quietly through the columns of the little round temple. I was pleased to see her.

"My dear, you're back. It seems like only a moment since —"

"It *was* rather a short life."

"Do tell."

"Well, you remember how I was trying to persuade them to let me do an experiment . . . It was only because I was proposing to stay just a short while that they let me go through with it."

"That's marvellous, you actually succeeded in cutting through all that mysterious red tape — it's simply marvellous."

"I wanted to see what existence would be like if you never got past that first attachment, you know, if you never had to give the mother up."

"But that's absurd —"

"I know, that's what everyone thinks. That consciousness and language and the whole structure of the psyche only come into being *through* that process of giving the mother up, and coping with the father's threat. Insofar as the pre-oedipal phase exists at all, it seems to be retrospective, something that only comes into awareness just at the moment you lose it forever. They think consciousness sounds the deathknell of that early relationship, it only exists as loss."

"You spend far too much time in the libraries of psychoanalysis. Really, conditions of existence are much better described in philosophy."

"But I wanted to test this theory out — by dying before I ever reached the oedipal phase. So it couldn't be retrospectively determined."

"And?"

"It's all nonsense. Admittedly, I didn't acquire language, or gender, or a sense of identity, but I was aware all the time, of everything around me. Maybe it's not consciousness, maybe it's a different kind of awareness. One that consciousness makes you forget."

"What were you aware of?"

"I could feel all my internal organs, I could feel the blood in my veins, and my heart pumping, and my gut digesting. It was very preoccupying, these sensations, I found it hard to focus on the outside world."

"Hang on a second, how old were you?"

"I killed myself when I was six months old."

"This is extraordinary. How?"

"I stopped breathing. It's quite common. You just, so to speak, forget to breathe."

"I'm deeply shocked. And you spent most of the time listening to your peristaltic waves?"

"Feeling them, feeling everything going on inside me in the most amazing detail. And being with, or without, the mother."

"And the father?"

"He was peripheral, when he wasn't absent. I wasn't bothered. I never made the connection that *he* was taking the mother away. Or that anyone was. Her absence seemed like a tragic act of fate, completely non-negotiable. Although I protested, of course. Rage is very pleasurable."

"And the mother?"

"Jeanie? I think she'll get over it. She'd predicted it anyway, she was always frightened her baby would die."

"Is that why you chose her?"

"In a sense she was prepared for it. More prepared than most."

"I think this is the most sadistic piece of sublunary research I've ever come across. I thought when you said you wanted to go back, to walk those chaotic, dirty streets —"

"In my mother's belly. I wanted to be inside her, and to know, somewhere deep in my bones, that this was it, there wasn't going to be anything more than this. The first love, and no other."

"And now?"

"Now I'm working on promotion to angel status."

"So you can interfere even more?"

"So I can communicate some of my discoveries. Being a baby is an awareness before division, before anything is divided up: sleep and waking, sexual sensations and others, thinking and feeling, inner and outer, pleasure and pain. The whole surface of my body, the dark volume inside me, were constantly surging with sensation, like perpetual electricity, pins and needles, but pleasurable. It's really great."

"That's why babies scream so much."

"That's the other side, you're at the mercy of things, not only beyond your control, but beyond you in every sense. Pure pain, no understanding."

"None of this seems very original to me, it's rather what I imagined infancy would be like."

"Yes, me too. But this is scientific."

"Rubbish. Corinne, you really are a disappointment."

"Don't be horrible to me."

"I'm sorry, my dear. I forgot you've never had a child of your own. It may be youthful high spirits, I suppose, and curiosity, but I think it's very cruel to those poor parents of yours . . ."

"You're a sentimentalist."

"I like the eighteenth century. Sentimental wasn't a dirty word in the eighteenth century."

"And scientific isn't a dirty word now."

"I don't call it science. I call it revenge."

"Possibly a combination of envy and revenge. But all science has an unconscious motivation."

"Enough of this. Let's walk down to the lake and look at the pyramids."

"All right."

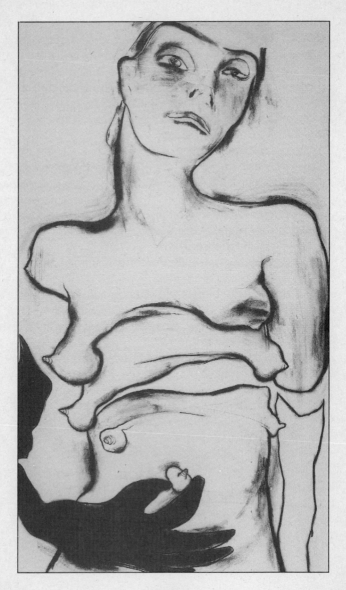

PRIDE

AGNES OWENS

PRIDE

"When Shankland Comes"

PRIDE

It was a raw March morning when Ivy came into the village hotel where she was employed as a cleaner. Sometimes she served in the public bar too, but at the moment she wasn't needed so often, for trade was always poor after the New Year. In summer, though, the hotel did well. It stood on the main road and was a good stopping point for tourists on their way to the mountains and lochs beyond. The village itself could be described as sleepy. Some folks said it was merely dull. On one side of the road was a long stretch of mansions near the hotel, and on the other a grocery store, adjacent to a small Scheme of neat one-storey council houses. Behind the Scheme stood a church dated eighteen ninety-four, refaced with pink modern brick. There was no school in the village. The kids, big and small, had to travel by local bus to the one in the small town of Blairmaddie, five miles away.

There were only two customers in the public bar: Geordie Forsyth the builder, and Sam Ferguson, who was elderly and toothless. Geordie Forsyth watched Ivy wipe the bar counter. She was a tall, angular-faced woman with an abundance of dark curling hair and a slim figure which was hidden under a green nylon overall. Though not young, being almost forty, older men — including Geordie Forsyth — still found her attractive. "Ye look fair scunnered," Geordie said.

"That's no crime," said Ivy, tossing her head. Her mind was on Dennett, her seventeen-year-old son. He had refused to get out of bed when she called him up for work, and he'd only just started the job on the farm two days ago. Admitted it was on the side and the wage was poor, but between that and his social security money you'd have thought he would be doing fine. When she called him a lazy bastard he'd said, well it wasn't his fault if he was a bastard, was it? The remark had rankled then, and it still did now.

"Gie us a smile," said Geordie, when she lifted his glass to wipe under it." "Ye're braw when ye smile."

"I'm no' in the mood for smilin'," said Ivy; nevertheless her mouth softened. She liked Geordie well enough. He wasn't bad looking in a coarse way and he had a steady job, which said a lot in his favour, but she didn't trust him. He was a hard drinker. Everybody knew that was why his wife had left him. Anyway she'd never had any time for men since Dennett was born.

"Whit she needs is a man," said old Sam, wheezing with laughter.

"That I don't need," said Ivy, rubbing away furiously. "Besides there's no men in this place, at least no' what I'd call one."

"Come roon the back and I'll soon show ye," said Geordie.

Sam laughed again. Ivy tutted and said to Geordie, "You should be at your buildin' instead of standin' here drinking. I don't know how you get away wi' it."

"Because I'm ma ain boss," said Geordie complacently, just as Jim Carr, the barman, came in.

"Hurry up wi' that counter so as I can get servin'," he told Ivy. Geordie put down his empty tumbler on the counter and walked out. Old Sam faded into the background, holding a glass which still contained an inch of beer.

"Who is there to serve?" snapped Ivy, and headed for the kitchen. It was almost ten o'clock and time for her cup of tea. Going down the hallway she met Walter Sproul, the manager. Although he barely glanced at her, she noted the bags under his eyes. Likely been on the bottle last night, she thought, and fighting with his wife. They could be heard first thing in the morning, either bawling at each other or thumping on their bed in a frenzy of love-making. Ivy despised Sproul and also that wife of his, who did absolutely nothing in the hotel except come down the stairs in the afternoon, her hair all frizzed up and her make-up thick, and drive off somewhere in her blue Mercedes. Of course when Shankland came it was a different story. Then you'd see her hovering behind Sproul as he spoke to Shankland with a smarmy smile on his face. Albert Shankland had been manager when Ivy first started work, twenty years ago. She had been taken on part-time as a waitress, then full-time, when they'd asked her to clean. The hotel had done well in those days, and it had always been a pleasure to work for Shankland. Eventually he bought up the hotel and then another one further south. When, soon afterwards, he'd moved south himself, appointing a new manager in his place, it had been a bitter blow. But that was a long time ago now, and many managers had come and gone before Sproul took over. Sproul, though, was the worst of the lot. She wished Shankland would come and pay the hotel one of his flying visits to study the books and give a pep talk to the staff. He always took her aside when he came, and spoke to her in a warm and friendly way. Once he even enquired about Dennett's health. "He's fine," she'd answered, not knowing what else to say.

In the big kitchen, Babs, the cook, was pouring out two cups of tea. Ivy began to spread butter thickly on a roll. "That Sproul gets on ma goat," Babs said.

"What's he done this time?" said Ivy.

"He says we'll have tae put less meat in the sandwiches." Staring hard at Ivy's roll, she added, "He'll go mad if he sees that."

"I'm no' takin' any meat," Ivy pointed out.

"I've got tae account for the butter as well," said Babs, her voice aggrieved.

Ivy shrugged, then sat up on a high stool with her back facing the table and her legs crossed. Babs frowned at the sight of Ivy's slim legs. Her own were short and fat. In fact she was fat all over, with a stomach that bulged out under her white overall. Her broad face was red from the heat of the kitchen. "By the way," she said, "are ye goin' tae the dance in the church hall on Saturday?"

Ivy wrinkled her nose slightly. "I don't know. They're gettin' awful stale nowadays."

"Ye always get a laugh at somethin', and the punch is free."

"I'm no' that desperate for a drink," said Ivy.

"There's nothin' much else happenin' in this dump," said Babs bitterly.

"If I go it means that Dennett's in the house by himsel' until dead late."

"Surely Dennett's auld enough to stay in by hissel'."

"I'll have to think about it," said Ivy, picturing Dennett bringing his pals in and drinking cans of lager.

Ivy was washing her cup when Jim burst into the kitchen and asked her to take the bar while he had some tea, since Betty, the lounge bar waitress, hadn't come in yet.

"I don't know how she's kept on," said Ivy. "She's always late."

"And she's that bloody cheeky wi' it tae," said Babs.

"Yous two are just jealous because she's sexy lookin'," Jim said.

Ivy and Babs laughed simultaneously. "She's as sexy lookin' as a coo lookin' ower a dyke," said Ivy.

There was nobody in the bar except old Sam, still holding his tumbler with its inch of beer.

"Finish that pint and get anither one," said Ivy. "This is no' a bus shelter you're staunin' in."

"I canny afford anither one," said Sam. "I've only got ma pension tae keep me."

"Aye, I know," said Ivy sighing. She was about to give him a free half pint when Betty came in, her blonde hair spiked at the top and long and flat at the back.

"I slept in," she explained, as old Sam gave her a startled look. He finished his beer and walked stiffly away.

"I'm sure that hair-do must have taken a good hour to fix," said Ivy.

"No' really," said Betty, "it's quite easy when ye know how."

Sensing that Betty was about to launch into a long explanation about why she'd slept in, Ivy said quickly, "Now that you're in I'm away to clean the toilets."

The day passed slowly for Ivy. Business was still poor in the afternoon apart from a few young lads from the Community Programme who came in to order coffee. She looked at them enviously as they came through the hotel door wearing their donkey jackets. She wished Dennett could have been one of them. Of course he was too young for the Community Programme, which mainly consisted of doing old folk's gardens. In the bad weather they didn't do much more than hang around the hotel entrance laughing loud and inanely, but at least they were obliged to get up in the morning. Dennett on the other hand, had still been in bed when she went home at lunchtime.

Sproul's wife had left as usual in her Mercedes and Sproul was prowling about the hotel like a pregnant cat, his face sullen and brooding, as if he wanted to find someone to lash out at. Ivy affected to look busy by polishing the hallway twice before she went through to the kitchen to scrub the big table. Babs had gone off duty at four o'clock, and the room was empty. Ivy stared up through the kitchen window at the tormented looking sky, thinking that it wouldn't be all that long until summer, when the place would be packed out. In the meantime she had only another hour to go.

On her way home she stopped at the grocery, which sold everything from a packet of pins to a jar of boiled mussels. The freezer near the door was filled with all sorts of frozen packets and half the counter was taken up with rolls, pies and doughnuts, all in separate cardboard boxes. Scarcely four people could stand inside the shop comfortably.

"My, it's a right cauld day," said Mrs Braithwaite, the owner, from behind the counter. She was a small stout elderly woman who always wore a hairnet over her blue perm.

"I'm fair roastin'," said Ivy, and went on to ask for two pies and a tin of beans.

"It'll be a' that hard work ye dae in the hotel," said Mrs Braithwaite. She put two pies in a poke, then, without turning round, lifted a tin of beans from the shelf behind her. The shop was so cramped that she scarcely needed to move an inch to put her hand on any item, except for the freezer, from which folk helped themselves. "I've heard the manager's no' very easy tae work for," she added.

"He's no' bad," said Ivy, reluctant to say anything that could get to Sproul's ears.

"They tell me the wages are no' very good," said Mrs Braithwaite, when Ivy handed over a pound note for the purchases.

"They're a lot better than what ye get off the social," said Ivy promptly.

"That's true," said Mrs Braithwaite, opening the till. "Though I've heard there's plenty on the social and workin' forbye." She looked directly at Ivy. "I don't think that's fair, dae you?"

"I don't suppose it is," said Ivy, wondering if the storekeeper knew that Dennett had worked two days on the farm. She asked for ten kingsize Regal before Mrs Braithwaite could pursue the subject any further, and headed for the door.

Outside, the wind blew cold in her face, but invigorating. Old autumn leaves stirred at the side of the pavement and in the distance she could see the peaks of the mountains covered in snow. She walked up the neat path of her council house noting the snowdrops under her window and reflecting that the village would be a nice enough place to stay in, if it wasn't for some of the folk.

When she came into the livingroom Dennett was sitting in the armchair facing the television with the gas fire turned up full.

"So, you've managed to get up then," she said, turning the fire low. He stretched his legs and kept his sharp profile fixed ahead. She noticed with distaste that his hair was uncombed. It lay on his shoulders light brown and straggly. "You might have washed yersel' at least," she muttered, as she went through to the kitchenette to put on the kettle. A minute later she was startled to see him towering above her looking anxious. "Did ye get my fags?" he asked.

"They're in my bag," she said, exasperated. "Do ye no' think it's terrible I should have to buy you fags and you'll no' even make an attempt to earn money to buy them yersel'?"

"I wisny feelin' well this mornin'," he said, ripping the cellophane from the packet. "I'll go tae work the morra."

"Well, ye'd better," she said, a bit mollified by this statement. "But mind," she added, "don't go near the store on your way to the farm. If auld Braithwaite thinks you're workin' she could report ye. She's that type."

"Aye" he said, then: "Are ye makin' chips?"

"No," she shouted, thinking that Dennett never seemed to give a damn about anything that really mattered.

"Did ye hear that Shankland's comin'?" Babs said to Ivy when she came into the hotel kitchen next morning.

"When?" said Ivy, trying not to look excited.

"Either Friday or Saturday," said Babs. She added morosely, "I hate when he comes."

"He's OK — a lot better than Sproul," said Ivy. "If Shankland has anythin' to say he tells ye fair and square, no' like Sproul wi' his snidy remarks for no good reason. Shankland doesny bother me."

"It's a' right for you," said Babs. "You're mair familiar wi' him than me."

"Whit dae ye mean 'familiar'?" said Ivy, her voice sharp.

"I only mean that you've known him longer than any of us. that's a'," said Babs, her eyes wide and innocent. She poured out the tea while Ivy buttered her roll heavily. "Anyway," she went on, "business is that bad I wouldny be surprised if he's up tae close the hotel. It's happenin' a' ower the place. I heard the hotel outside Blairmaddie's tae close and it only opened three years ago."

Ivy made no comment on this, inwardly seething at the use of the word "familiar". It looked as though Babs was jealous of her long acquaintanceship with Shankland. She'd have to be careful of what she said to her in future. When she was washing her cup at the sink Babs said, "Are ye still no' goin' tae the dance?"

"Definitely no'," snapped Ivy, marching off to dust and hoover the lounge, although she didn't think it would need much cleaning since it hadn't been opened since Monday.

Thursday was cold, but bright. The hotel was surprisingly busy with families tempted out for the day by the early spring sun, and some of the wealthy retired locals from the big houses. The lounge was opened and there were six men standing in the public bar, including Geordie Forsyth who came in every day anyway. Ivy was asked to serve in the bar while Betty did the lounge. All this and the fact that Dennett had got out of his bed and gone to his job at the farm put Ivy in a good mood. Jim hummed tunes under his breath as he pulled the pints, and Sproul walked between the lounge and the bar with his face less haunted looking than usual. Only Babs in the kitchen was grumbling when Ivy dashed in for a quick cup of tea; she hadn't time for a roll. "If it's goin' tae be as busy as this," she said, "I'll need extra help."

"I thought you said the hotel might be closin' down," Ivy laughed.

"If it's no' one way it's another," Babs shouted as Ivy dashed off, "Don't forget one swallow doesny make a summer."

Ivy didn't go home for lunch, since she had a lot of catching up to do with the cleaning. She took a snack in the kitchen, and then carried on with all her other jobs: the washing, the hoovering and dusting, the polishing. It was hard going, she thought, but it was worth it to see the place so busy. Maybe from now on business would pick up and everyone would be in a better mood. When she got home at half past five after stopping at the store to buy milk, bread and cheese, her face fell. Dennett sat in the chair facing the television with the gas fire turned up full.

"I thought ye didny stop until six," she said, blinking nervously.

"I've been sacked," he said.

"Sacked?" she said, throwing her message bag on the couch and sinking down beside it.

"Aye, sacked," he said defiantly. "It wis because I never came in yesterday. I've been in here since nine in the mornin'."

"I knew this would happen," she said bitterly.

Dennett's voice was equally bitter. "I'm glad I wis sacked. You don't know whit it's like tae muck out dung all day, and then havin' tae eat your piece wi' yer haunds all smelly, and no' even a drap o' tea to wash it down. Anyway it wisny a real job, I'd only have got paid in washers."

"Did you get yer two days' money then?"

"Naw, he said I wis tae come back on Saturday."

"And I bet like hell you bloody well won't," said Ivy, her temper rising. "And here's me workin' my pan in to keep you in meals and fags and put a good face on everythin' and tryin' to keep decent and there you are tellin' me you're above muckin' out byres . . . Well I don't particularly like bein' a cleaner and gettin' paid in washers either, but I have to do it to keep a roof above our heids."

Dennett sneered, "That's up tae you."

Enraged, Ivy jumped up from the couch and slapped him on the cheek. Dennett confronted her with eyes blazing. For a second she thought he was going to slap her back, but he only stared at her madly for a moment before he rushed out of the room. She heard his bedroom door slam hard, then silence. She sat down on the couch again, drained, vowing to herself that she would tell Dennett to get out. He was old enough to take care of himself, after all; why should she put up with his laziness and cheek? He could get himself a room or a bed and breakfast somewhere in Blairmaddie, and come to think of it Blairmaddie would suit him better, being full of licensed grocers and pubs.

Knowing him he'd likely just drift around spending his social money on booze or even dope: she'd heard there were junkies galore there. At least, she thought angrily, if he's out of the way he can't give me a showing up in the village. She sat for a while thinking of what could happen to Dennett in Blairmaddie or some other bigger place beyond. But she could never do it, of course. He was too feckless. It was quite beyond her to put him out at seventeen. Besides, he wouldn't go easily, and after all he might get a job with the Community Programme next September when he was eighteen. Sighing, she stood up and went through to the kitchenette to make some tea and toasted cheese. It was all she felt fit to cook. Ten minutes later she shouted from the livingroom, "Dennett, come and get your supper." When he came through he peered at the plate on the work top, saying in a perplexed manner, "Toasted cheese? How did ye no' make chips for a change?"

On Friday it snowed and again there was hardly anybody in the bar except Geordie Forsyth who was at one of the tables in the small room, deep in discussion with two of the brickies he employed. He hardly glanced at Ivy when she came in to clean, which annoyed her in a way, especially when she had taken extra pains with her hair, brushing it hard so that it fell smoothly round her face, as well as putting on a touch of eye-shadow and lipstick. Although all this was for Shankland's benefit, she'd expected a compliment or two from Geordie. Betty came in right on time for once, and Ivy didn't doubt that it was because she too expected Shankland at any minute. Jim stood behind Betty polishing the glasses intently.

The morning passed and Shankland did not show up, nor was there any sign of Sproul in the hotel. This seemed strange to Ivy but she didn't remark on it, not even to Babs. In fact, they had scarcely a word to say to each other during the tea break. It was as if they had mutually decided to fall out.

Ivy came back home at lunch feeling thoroughly disgruntled. She was taken aback to see Dennett up and fully clothed, eating toast and scambled egg. Then she remembered that this was his Giro day.

"There's some egg left in the pot," he said obligingly.

"Thanks," she said curtly, thinking he'd have done better to make a slice of toast to go with it. Before she left she reminded him to leave his money on the sideboard after he had cashed the Giro at Braithwaite's store.

"I always dae," he answered with a touch of indignation.

In the afternoon when she took the hoover into the lounge she was surprised to see Sproul's wife standing behind the small lounge bar. "Don't bother hoovering," she told Ivy. "The carpet's clean enough. Just separate the tables. They're far too close together."

"I always hoover the carpet whether it's clean or no'." Ivy said hotly. "That's how it's in such good condition."

"Nonsense," said Sproul's wife. "Just do as I say."

"Wait a minute," said Ivy, her eyes blazing. "Since when have you taken charge?"

Sproul's wife said tartly, "As from today, I'm in charge of the lounge." As Ivy stared at her in disbelief, Sproul's wife, her lips cyclamen pink and smiling, added, "if you don't believe me, ask my husband when he comes in."

"I'll no' bother seein' your husband," Ivy retorted, "I'll wait tae Shankland comes in. It seems to me he's the main one to see."

"Do you think so?" said Sproul's wife, assuming an astonished expression. "I'd hardly credit that, when my husband is paid to manage the hotel. However, if you want to see Mr Shankland you'll have to wait until tomorrow. He's down at Blairmaddie at the moment discussing business with my husband in the Riverbank Hotel. He thought it better to stay there for the night on account of the roads being so bad up here with the snow."

Ivy gave Sproul's wife one black look, then turned on her heel, trailing the hoover behind her.

"What about separating the tables," Sproul's wife called, but Ivy was off into the toilet to try and calm herself down.

On a Friday at tea-time the store was always busy, mainly with women rushing in at the last minute after collecting their husband's wages. Although there was less rushing in nowadays than there used to be, it was still busy enough to make Ivy fume with impatience as she waited at the end of the queue. She wanted to get home quickly to make sure that her share of Dennett's Giro was lying on the sideboard, but over and above that, she had been completely thrown into confusion by her encounter with Sproul's wife. It seemed to her as she waited that Mrs Braithwaite was chatting longer than ever with the customers. When finally her turn came, she asked for bread, potatoes and half a pound of sausages in a clipped voice. But this didn't prevent the storekeeper informing her that Dennett had just been in to cash his Giro. As Ivy nodded and opened her purse, Mrs Braithwaite added, "It's a pity he canny get work, a big strong fella like that."

Ivy was stung into saying, "There's no work to be had, is there?"

"I don't know," said Mrs Braithwaite deliberately. "There's some that widny take a job if it was under their very nose."

Ivy grabbed her change from Mrs Braithwaite's fat fingers and marched out past the queue that had formed behind her.

When she went in through the front door she heard Dennett running the tap in the bathroom. He usually celebrated his Giro day with a bath and a hair wash before going out with his pals for a night in Blairmaddie. She put the kettle on then checked to see if her money was on the sideboard. It was — the whole twenty-five pounds of it. His dinner was on the plate when he came into the kitchen, rubbing his hair with a towel, his face pink and shiny.

"Good," he said. "Chips."

"I'm glad somethin' pleases you," she said drily, following him into the livingroom. Dennett stuffed chips into his mouth, gazing dreamily at the television. Ivy picked at her meal half-heartedly. Before she lifted the dishes to wash them she told Dennett to mind and go up to the farm on Saturday and get the money owed to him.

"Aye — so I wull," he said reluctantly, frowning, as if he had no intention of going at all. Then he stood up and went into his bedroom. Within seconds the insistent beat of some pop group pounded on her ear drums. She debated whether to go through and tell him to turn the record down. Instead she took a pair of ear plugs from a drawer in the kitchen cabinet and sat down on the couch, staring blankly at a television she couldn't hear. An hour later he peeped into the livingroom to tell her that he was away. She took the ear plugs out and told him not to be late.

"Aye, so I wull," he said. She knew she was wasting her breath.

On Saturday rain turned the snow on the pavements to slush. Ivy came into the public bar wearing a blue woollen dress minus her nylon apron. She had decided to look good for Shankland, but when Jim turned to her and said, "For a second I thought you wir Sproul's wife," she began to wonder if the dress was a mistake.

"I should hope no'," she muttered, dying to ask him if Shankland had come in last night, but her pride kept her silent. She only asked if Sproul was around.

"No' yit," he answered, pulling a face as if something was happening that only he knew about. When she began to wipe the shelves he said in low voice, "Sproul's wife is takin' over the lounge."

"So I heard," said Ivy. "Well, maybe it's time she did something for her keep."

"Looks as if there's gaun to be a lot mair changes," said Jim darkly.

Curtly Ivy replied, "It's all one tae me, I'm only the cleaner, thank God." Jim turned away to serve one of the men who had come forward from a youngish crowd who sat at a table. Every Saturday morning they came in, deafening the place with their loud aggressive talk. Ivy was glad to get out of the bar whenever they arrived.

"Would ye like to gie us a hand?" Jim asked her when another two of the men came forward to the counter.

"I've got a lot to do," said Ivy hurrying away: Betty would be in any minute and she'd be overjoyed to serve that boisterous lot.

"That's a nice dress ye've on," Babs said to her in the kitchen, evidently prepared to be friendly.

"Actually it's quite an old one," said Ivy.

"It doesny look it," said Babs. "How have ye no' got yer apron on? It'll get a' dirty."

"I forgot to bring it. Anyway it doesny matter if it gets dirty," said Ivy impatiently.

"Here, d'ye know that Sproul's wife's in the lounge?" said Babs, handing Ivy a cup of tea and a roll which she explained was already buttered.

"Thanks," said Ivy, suspecting the roll would be buttered thin. "She telt me herself yesterday."

"Did she?" said Babs, her eyes wide. "You must be well in. Naebody tells me anythin' except when it's history."

"I wouldn't worry about it," said Ivy. "There's always bound to be changes at some time."

"Aye, but changes are never for the best nowadays," said Babs.

"Let's look on the bright side for once," said Ivy, feeling anything but bright. She suddenly had a premonition: either Shankland wasn't going to come in at all, or maybe he had been in last night and gone away again. So if Sproul's wife was going to take over the lounge, where did that leave her? If Betty had only the public bar to do it meant that they wouldn't need her to serve at all and there definitely wasn't enough cleaning to justify her hours from nine to five. And if they cut her hours, she might as well be on the dole. She'd have to talk to Sproul about it immediately.

Suddenly Babs said, "Are you still no' goin' tae the dance?"

"I've already told you I'm no'," said Ivy sharply.

"Then I don't think I'll go either," said Babs. "I hate goin' in the door masel'."

"Don't then," said Ivy. She felt like screaming.

Later, when she was coming out of the toilet, Betty told her in a casual way that she'd heard Shankland was coming in the afternoon. Ivy brightened up at that. She decided that there was no need to see Sproul. Shankland would allay her fears. So what if Sproul's wife was managing the lounge? She could come to terms with that as long as they didn't cut her hours.

When she got home at lunchtime she looked in at Dennett's room to see if he was all right. Heaven knows what time he'd come home last night, and in what condition. When she'd left this morning she had been so preoccupied by the affairs of the hotel that she'd forgotten all about him. She found him lying on his back, snoring his head off, his long legs sticking out from under the blankets. "Dennett," she called, but he continued to snore. When she called again, "Do ye want something to eat?" he grunted "Naw," and turned on his side. She studied him for a while, almost envying his complete disregard for anyone but himself. He had no talent, no ambition and no pride, yet he looked so happy lying there with that slight smile on his lips.

The afternoon wore on and still there was no sign of Shankland. Sproul passed her once or twice as she was polishing the woodwork in the corridor, and ducked his head in an embarrassed way which made her wonder. But when Jim handed over her pay envelope at half past four she found out why. Inside was two weeks' money and a letter saying that due to increased overheads and poor trade, the management regretted that they no longer required her services. However, as soon as trade picked up they would send for her again.

Ivy scanned the letter twice to make sure she had read correctly. Then chalkfaced, she went off in search of Sproul. She found him behind the lounge bar standing close to his wife. They were studying a ledger and they looked conspiratorial. Ivy thrust the letter under Sproul's nose and said, "You canny do this to me."

Sproul and his wife looked up at her with pained expressions. Sproul said, "I'm very sorry about this, but . . ."

"Never mind bein' sorry," Ivy interrupted. "I'm goin' to see Shankland. When will he be in?"

Sproul's wife shoved her face forward. "He won't be in," she said spitefully. "He's already spoken to us about everything. Isn't that right, Walter?"

"Yes," Sproul said heavily.

Ivy's head swam. She said faintly, "He canny know about this. Shankland would never sack me."

"It was his instructions," said Sproul.

"You're lyin'," said Ivy. "Give me his address and I'll get in touch wi' him myself."

Sproul and his wife exchanged weary glances. "Look Ivy," said Sproul, "if you want to see him, try the church hall round about ten o'clock. He and his wife have been invited to the dance as special guests, but I can assure you that letter was written on his instructions."

"I still don't believe you," said Ivy, turning away to hide the tears in her eyes. A minute later she put on her coat and walked out of the hotel without saying a word to anyone.

Prompt on ten Ivy was inside the church hall, still wearing her blue woollen dress and fortified by two glasses of port from the bottle which had been in her sideboard since the New Year. She was dismayed to see that hardly anyone had turned up, apart from the minister and some church elders waiting by the door; the minister's wife and her cronies stood at the far end of the hall beside a table spread with food. The band sat on a platform in a corner near the entrance, wearing maroon shirts and dark suits. It was the same band that played every year, its members middle-aged and bespectacled. Hesitantly Ivy went over to the table and, for want of anything better to do, helped herself to a sandwich and a glass of punch from the big fruit bowl in the centre.

"How nice to see you, Ivy," said the minister's wife, smiling horsily.

"Likewise, I'm sure," said Ivy. She took a gulp of the punch and shuddered.

"Strong, isn't it?" said the minister's wife. "There's a bottle of brandy in it. I made it myself."

"It's very good," said Ivy, forcing a smile. She added brightly, "There's no' many turned up though."

"They'll be fortifyin' themselves in the hotel," said Mrs Braithwaite, who wore pink gingham and for once had no hairnet on.

"Do you mind if I sit down?" said Ivy. She was beginning to feel dizzy from drinking the strong punch on top of the port. She went over to the bench against the wall and sat there sipping from her glass until she calmed down a bit. A crowd of men and women thrust through the door like cattle from a stockade, and the band began to play a slow foxtrot. The minister and his wife were the first on the floor, dancing awkwardly, their faces strained. Ivy decided to have just one more glass of punch. It would while away the time until Shankland arrived. Although by now her head was so foggy that quite honestly she didn't really care whether he came or not. When she turned round from the table she saw Babs sailing towards her like a gigantic balloon in her wide orange dress.

"I thought you wereny comin'," said Babs indignantly, helping herself to a sausage roll. With crumbs falling from her mouth, she added: "Is it true ye've got the sack?"

"Is that what you heard?" said Ivy, taking a gulp of punch.

"Well, is it true?" Babs persisted.

"Nothing that's ever said in this place is true." Ivy pointed to the bowl of punch. "Try some of that. It's strong stuff. There's a whole bottle of brandy in it." She heard herself laugh foolishly.

"It seems tae be," said Babs, staring hard at Ivy. Then she walked off to talk to the minister's wife, leaving Ivy on her own.

Geordie Forsyth came up from behind then, and asked her for a dance. She was vaguely surprised to see him so smart in a grey pin-striped suit. "Right," she said, grateful for the rescue. As they waltzed round the hall she tripped over his feet, feeling quite giddy.

"Steady on," said Geordie. He pulled her close, his hand pressing her waist. If it hadn't been for the half bottle in Geordie's pocket jamming hard into her hip, she would happily have floated round the hall for the rest of the night. When the dance ended, Geordie asked her if she'd like to come outside for a wee nip of whisky.

"I don't know . . ." she began. And then she saw Shankland standing in the doorway. With him was a small, plump, matronly woman in a black lace dress. Shankland was shaking hands with the minister, his heavy-jowled face lit by a smile. He was a big man with a thick waist. He had never been handsome, exactly, but you could tell he attracted attention wherever he went.

Without thinking, Ivy rushed forward. "Mr Shankland," she said, tugging at his sleeve, "can I have a word with you? It's very important."

Shankland turned round, frowning. "Later, Ivy. Can't you see my wife and I are talking to the minister?"

His wife, who as far as Ivy could see hadn't been talking at all, looked her up and down with suspicion.

"I'm sorry," said Ivy, "but Sproul's sacked me from the hotel and I've been waitin' for you to come in." The words came out slurred. She broke off, sick at heart at Shankland's expression.

"Yes, I'm sorry it had to happen," he said guardedly. "But you see, it was either that or closing down the hotel altogether. However, if the place does better in the summer we'll send for you again, don't worry on that score." And with that he turned back to the minister, who had been listening anxiously.

Suddenly Ivy's rage erupted. "You mean to say," she said, her voice rising, "that you were the one who sacked me, after all these years? All these years I've been loyal and kept my mouth shut?"

Shankland scarcely looked at her. "Go away, Ivy," he said wearily. "You're drunk."

"Yes, do go and sit down, Ivy," the minister pleaded. "You're not your usual self. Perhaps it's the punch. I told my wife not to put in so much brandy."

"What do you mean — 'kept your mouth shut'?" asked Shankland's wife, her face puckering.

"Don't listen to her," Shankland said. "She's just upset and a bit drunk. That's all there is to it." He led his wife towards the table, bending over her slightly, while the minister followed close behind.

Ivy stood for a moment, dazed, her mind fuddled by the slow monotonous rhythm of the band. She noticed Geordie Forsyth dancing with Babs and looking genteel. A taste of bile was in her mouth and her head was in a turmoil. She saw Shankland turn his back on her and offer his wife a sandwich from a plate. Then all at once her mind was made up. She rushed across to the table.

"That's no' all there is to it!" she said in a voice loud and clear. "What about Dennett, my son and yours, whom I've kept for seventeen years without a penny off ye? I took the blame on myself, aye, they say it's always the woman to blame, don't they. But since you think so little of me I might as well admit in front of everybody here that you're Dennett's father. I think ye owe me something for that."

"You're crazy!" said Shankland, with a furtive look at his wife. Her face had turned white as a sheet. All around the table a hush had fallen, and people were staring. He grabbed his wife's elbow. "Let's get out of here," he whispered.

The small woman stood her ground, trembling. "Leave me alone," she said.

Shankland tugged at her urgently. "Come on."

And then his wife's arm jerked up and her eyes went blank and she threw the glass of punch straight into Shankland's face.

"Oh dear," said the minister, his hands fluttering in the air, and someone laughed. There were a few more titters. Then Shankland turned and marched towards the door, his wife following a yard or two behind.

Ivy clutched at the table for support.

"Go ower and sit down," Mrs Braithwaite said in a surprisingly kind voice. "I'll see if I can get a cup of tea from somewhere." She glared at the minister's wife. "That punch bowl's been a bloody curse!"

"I'm okay," said Ivy, smiling wanly.

"I'm awful sorry," said the minister's wife with an apologetic look at Ivy. "I shouldn't have put so much brandy in."

"Don't worry yourself, I quite enjoyed it." Ivy walked over to the bench by the wall and sat down. Geordie Forsyth and Babs came off the dance floor, red-faced and dripping with sweat.

"Have you been sittin' here a' night?" Babs sounded concerned.

"No' really," said Ivy.

"I thought I saw Shankland come in."

"So he did," said Ivy. "He's away now."

"Did he say anythin'? I mean, about you gettin' the sack?"

"No' as much as I said to him."

Geordie took the half bottle from his pocket. "Do any of youse ladies want a wee nip?"

"No' straight frae the bottle," said Babs, aghast.

"I'll take one," said Ivy, putting the bottle to her mouth.

"Will ye look at her!" Babs said. "To think she's aye sae proud and ladylike."

"No' any more," said Ivy. The rough whisky trickled down her throat. She was about to tilt the bottle again when a sudden thought stopped her. Dennett. It wasn't as if she only had herself to consider, after all. Likely he'd be in on his own, watching the television, since he never had any money left on a Saturday to go anywhere. Aye, Dennett. Somebody had to set him an example, didn't they, and she'd been doing it for years so she wasn't about to stop now. She handed the bottle back to Geordie and struggled to her feet. "I think I'll go home now."

"Away, it's still early," said Geordie, looking at his watch.

"I must get home," Ivy said firmly. "I've left Dennett in himsel' and he's no' to be trusted."

"There goes an awfy determined woman," said Geordie, as he and Babs watched her leave.

"The trouble wi' Ivy," said Babs, "is that she's aye been too big for her boots, and now she's been sacked she canny take it." She sniffed loudly. "If you ask me, it serves her right."

OTHER TITLES
· FROM ·
SERPENT'S TAIL

JOHN AGARD *Mangoes and Bullets*
JORGE AMADO *Dona Flor and Her Two Husbands*
DAVID BRADLEY *The Chaneysville Incident*
MICHEL DEL CASTILLO *The Disinherited*
ANDRÉE CHEDID *From Sleep Unbound*
ANDRÉE CHEDID *The Sixth Day*
ILYA EHRENBURG *The Life of the Automobile*
WAGUIH GHALI *Beer in the Snooker Club*
WILLIAM GOYEN *Had I a Hundred Mouths*
OSCAR HIJUELOS *Our House in the Last World*
LANGSTON HUGHES *Selected Poems*
CHARLES JOHNSON *The Sorcerer's Apprentice*
WARD JUST *The American Ambassador*
ISMAIL KADARE *Chronicle in Stone*
CLAUDE McKAY *Banana Bottom*
VAZQUEZ MONTALBAN *Murder in the Central
Committee*
VAZQUEZ MONTALBAN *Southern Seas*
DEA TRIER MØRCH *Winter's Child*
DEA TRIER MØRCH *Evening Star*
DANIEL MOYANO *The Devil's Trill*
HERTA MÜLLER *The Passport*
KENZABURO OE *The Silent Cry*
J. J. PHILLIPS *Mojo Hand*
MARIA THOMAS *Antonia Saw the Oryx First*
TOM WAKEFIELD *The Variety Artistes*

NON FICTION

M   A   S   K   S

Leslie Dick
WITHOUT FALLING

'A debut of great conviction and profound originality.'
NEW MUSICAL EXPRESS

'A boldly overambitious novel . . . promising stuff.'
BLITZ

'Thankfully a million miles from the rosily worthy world of seventies feminist fiction.'
WOMEN'S REVIEW

'It is rare these days to find a novel which is so fresh, harsh, exciting and funny.'   NEW STATESMAN

'In a literary culture dominated by gentility and middlebrowism, *Without Falling* is itself something of a bomb.'
LONDON REVIEW OF BOOKS

160 pages £4.95 (paper)

Luisa Valenzuela
THE LIZARD'S TAIL

'Luisa Valenzuela has written a wonderfully free ingenious novel about sensuality and power and death, the "I" and literature. Only a Latin American could have written *The Lizard's Tail*, but there is nothing like it in contemporary Latin American literature.'   SUSAN SONTAG

'By knotting together the writer's and the subject's fates, Valenzuela creates an extraordinary novel whose thematic ferocity and baroque images explore a political situation too exotically appalling for reportage.'   THE OBSERVER

'Its exotic, erotic forces seduce with consummate, subliminal force.'   BLITZ

'Don't classify it as another wonder of "magic realism": read, learn and fear.'   TIME OUT

'*The Lizard's Tail* will probably sell far fewer copies than Isabel Allende's inferior *Of Love and Shadows*, and that is a great pity. [It] is a wild adventurous book . . . a gripping and challenging read.'
                                      THIRD WORLD QUARTERLY

288 pages £7.95 (paper)

Janice Eidus
FAITHFUL REBECCA

'Eidus's style is witty and unpretentious, with a surrealistic edge that is never out of control. Her descriptions of Rebecca's fantasies and sensations are sensuous and erotic, with an amused awareness that her heroine, a fully paid-up member of the Me Generation, is forever trying out a succession of roles.' SUNDAY TIMES

'Funny, clever, sexy, tender and tough, a real find.' NEW STATESMAN & SOCIETY

'A highly entertaining and refreshing book.' THE PINK PAPER

'Moving and erotic.' TLS

176 pages £5.95

Dea Trier Mørch
WINTER'S CHILD

'You can almost smell the heavy perfume of birth, a mixture of blood and sweet milk. Evocative and powerful writing, it rings true to women's experience.'
SHEILA KITZINGER

'Simply wonderful.' CITY LIMITS

'How I wish that *Winter's Child* had been written [when I was pregnant] . . . I came away from this book with a clearer perception of my own experience.' WOMEN'S REVIEW

Illustrated by the author
272 pages £4.95 (paper)

EVENING STAR

'This is a remarkable novel, dealing squarely and unsentimentally with death.' SUNDAY TIMES

'Superbly illustrated by the author's own woodcuts, which are simple and black and bear a kind of dignified beauty amply in keeping with the mood of this book.' CITY LIFE

Illustrated by the author
272 pages £6.95 (paper)